W9-BMP-576

"Did you know that flowers speak their own language?"

When he gave her a look, she explained, "For instance, the red rose means beauty and love," which was probably why she loved red roses the best.

"What about yellow?" Daniel asked.

"Jealousy and envy. And daisies stand for innocence," she added.

"How do you know this?"

"A book called *The Language of Flowers*. It was published in the 1800s. My mother has a copy." Greer adored the book. She'd spent many a drama-filled, teenaged evenings reading the poetry and studying the meanings.

"Remind me to check with you before I send you flowers."

"Are you planning on sending me flowers?"

He grinned at her. "Maybe."

She smiled happily. Despite her years designing and decorating floats, she'd never gotten over her love of flowers. She inhaled their scent and turned to him, and he surprised her by sliding his arms around her and pulling her close for a kiss.

His lips were warm and seductive against hers. And for a second she was too surprised to respond.

SEP 2016

Dear Reader,

Greer Courtland has been designing Rose Parade floats since high school. When Daniel Torres enters into a friendly wager with a friend on who could win the best trophy, she does her best to provide him with the winning float design. Little did they know that this competition would lead to a lifetime of love and happiness. Join Greer and Daniel as they march through the twists and turns of passion and create their own little parade with the language of love.

The Rose Parade on New Year's Day is one of America's grandest traditions. With dozens of floats decorated in flowers, marching bands and drill teams, it's an incredible spectacle. Viewers camp out on Colorado Boulevard to get the best curbside seats while knowledgeable TV commentators provide background information. This year, Bob Eubanks and Stephanie Edwards, who have been the cornerstones of the parade commentary for over thirty years, announced their retirement. Their witty, intelligent comments will be much missed.

Much love,

Miriam and Jackie

BLOSSOMS OF *Love*

J.M. Jeffries

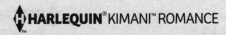

HARLEQUIN® KIMANI™ ROMANCE

If you purchased this book without a cover you should be aware
that this book is stolen property. It was reported as "unsold and
destroyed" to the publisher, and neither the author nor the
publisher has received any payment for this "stripped book."

Recycling programs
for this product may
not exist in your area.

ISBN-13: 978-0-373-86467-6

Blossoms of Love

Copyright © 2016 by Miriam A. Pace and Jacqueline S. Hamilton

All rights reserved. The reproduction, transmission or utilization of this
work in whole or in part in any form by any electronic, mechanical or
other means, now known or hereinafter invented, including xerography,
photocopying and recording, or in any information storage or retrieval
system, is forbidden without written permission. For permission please
contact Harlequin Kimani, 225 Duncan Mill Road, Toronto, Ontario
M3B 3K9, Canada.

This is a work of fiction. Names, characters, places and incidents are
either the product of the author's imagination or are used fictitiously,
and any resemblance to actual persons, living or dead, business establishments,
events or locales is entirely coincidental.

® and TM are trademarks of Harlequin Enterprises Limited or its corporate
affiliates. Trademarks indicated with ® are registered in the United States
Patent and Trademark Office, the Canadian Intellectual Property Office and in
other countries.

For questions and comments about the quality of this book please contact us
at CustomerService@Harlequin.com.

Printed in U.S.A.

™ www.Harlequin.com

Jackie and Miriam live in Southern California. When they aren't writing, Jackie is trying to take a nap and Miriam plays with her grandchildren. Jackie thought she wanted to be a lawyer until she met Miriam and decided to be a writer instead. Miriam always wanted to be a writer from her earliest childhood when she taught herself to read at age four. Both are avid readers and can usually be found with their noses in a book, or, now that it's the twenty-first century, an e-reader. Check out their blog at jmjeffries.com.

Books by J.M. Jeffries

Harlequin Kimani Romance

Virgin Seductress
My Only Christmas Wish
California Christmas Dreams
Love Takes All
Love's Wager
Bet on My Heart
Drawing Hearts
Blossoms of Love

Visit the Author Profile page at
Harlequin.com for more titles.

To all the loyal volunteers who show up year after year
to help decorate the floats for the Rose Parade.
They put in long hours, and the rewards are seeing
their chosen floats drive down Colorado Boulevard.
Who else can say, "I helped decorate that float"?

Acknowledgments

Jackie: For Miriam, because she puts up with me
even though she doesn't have regular mayonnaise
in the house.

Miriam: For Jackie. I like mayo made with olive oil.
It's healthy and doesn't taste as nasty as she says.

Prologue

Daniel Torres sat in his parents' large family room, his brothers situated around him, along with his best friend, Logan Pierce. The room had been the center of his life since birth, large enough to accommodate Daniel, his four brothers and two sisters. Today, as was tradition, they were all there, except for Nina, who, with her new husband, had decided to stay in Reno. His other sister, Lola, was sick and comfortably ensconced in her childhood bedroom so their mom could take care of her.

As a child, Daniel and his friends used to camp out in this room, and he had fond memories of making popcorn, sharing a stolen beer and watching movies. These days it looked different. Several years ago, his parents installed a whole-wall entertainment system with a superlarge TV, surround sound and two rows of home-theater recliners. Off to one side was a tiny galley kitchen, where his mother bustled about, making sure everyone had enough food. As though anyone would starve in this house.

Now the group sat in the leather recliners watching as the Rose Parade wound its way down Colorado Boulevard. The watching of the Rose Parade had been a Torres tradition ever since his parents had sponsored a float years ago.

Logan nudged Daniel's elbow. "What are we competing on this year?"

Daniel wasn't quite certain how they'd gotten into this yearly competition, but somehow it had grown into the loser donating $100,000 to the winner's favorite charity. "No more jumping frogs, rolling cheese wheels or fighting thumbs."

"You want something serious this time?" Logan's eyebrows shot up in surprise.

Daniel thought about that for a moment. "Not serious, but not weird." Logan excelled in weird. That was part of the former pro football player's nightly newscast, along with sports. Daniel had his own show—a morning edition that was more entertainment than news.

"What do you consider not serious, but not weird?" Logan took a long drink of his morning coffee. He was a night owl, while Daniel was usually up by four in the morning and at the station by four thirty to get ready for his show.

"A football game is serious. Anything that involves

Spam is weird." The first float appeared on the screen with a banner underneath it claiming it was the winner of the Sweepstakes Trophy. "I've got an idea. Let's sponsor a float for the Rose Parade."

Daniel looked at his friend, once again struck by their different appearances. Logan looked like the typical California surfer with his sun-bleached blond hair, deep-set blue eyes and muscular body. Daniel was the product of his black Brazilian father whose own father emigrated from Bermuda and a mother whose ancestry was unknown. His eyes were a deep amber, his skin the color of his favorite mocha Frappuccino, and he was more lean and slender than muscular.

Logan pointed at the screen. "You mean a fancy float like that? With flowers?"

"Why not?"

"What would be the stakes?"

"The usual—your charity or mine."

Daniel had sponsored the Wounded Warrior Project for several years. Logan supported the American Red Cross. "We have to win a trophy."

"There are like twenty trophies," Logan said.

"The Sweepstakes is the most prestigious," Nicholas, Daniel's fraternal twin brother, put in.

"I think you should try for the Princesses' Trophy. It's for the most beautiful float," Sebastian, another brother, threw out.

"Remember that dog pool a couple of years ago? That float had everything." Nicholas's eyes glazed over with the memory. He loved animals and would adopt every stray he found if he didn't have such a demanding job as a choreographer for Broadway musicals. He'd recently been asked to bring his talents back to Los Angeles for a *Dancing with the Stars* clone.

"I think you should try for the Bob Hope Humor Trophy. That's my favorite," Matteus said. He was the only Torres who had chosen to move away from the family's heritage and into a profession outside the entertainment industry. He was a cop in West Hollywood.

Everyone started to weigh in on their preferences. Sebastian, the eldest Torres brother, supported the Governor's Trophy. Even as he watched TV, his flexible magician's fingers shuffled a deck of cards. He never went anywhere without them, it seemed to Daniel, who was used to Sebastian's constant card tricks.

"I was joking about the float," Daniel said when the arguments wound down.

"But I like it," Logan said. "It's different. It's splashy. We could have a ton of fun with this."

Daniel watched the TV for a few moments, admiring the different floats. His thoughts churned and his imagination went into overdrive. He could really promote this, getting a lot of mileage for their charities. His station would probably contribute something, and, because their respective audiences seemed to enjoy their lighthearted competition, they could set up an independent account for private donations, as well.

"Okay," Daniel finally said. "We can do this."

Logan punched his arm. "Sure we can."

Daniel got up to fix himself another cup of coffee and snagged a cookie off the plate his mother had just refilled. Ideas spun in his head. While he was great with promotion ideas, he didn't know anything about floats.

"Is that a glint of panic in your eyes?" Manny Torres, Daniel's father, said with a smile.

"What do I know about floats?" Daniel asked as he poured cream into his coffee.

"Not a thing."

"How am I going to pull this off? Three years in a row, I've lost this competition with Logan. Look at him. He's gloating. In his head, I've already written a check to his charity."

Manny put a hand on Daniel's arm. "Son, there are times in a man's life, no matter how grown he is, when he needs to listen to his papa."

Daniel studied his father's face. "You have a guy?"

"Yes." Manny's smile grew. "Consider it done."

"What about Logan?"

Manny glanced at Logan, fondness in his eyes. "I love Logan as though he was my own, but you come first."

Logan's head was bent over his iPhone, his fingers flying over the touch screen. He looked up and glanced back at Daniel. "Did you know there are a number of companies who do nothing but build floats for the Rose Parade?"

Daniel shook his head. "I had no idea."

Logan waved his phone. "May the best man win." He put his phone to his ear and got up, walking away to a quieter corner. "I know it's New Year's Day, but I need you to get me an appointment on the fourth with Steinmen and Sons." He paused, listening, no doubt, to his assistant, who seemed to be on call 24/7. "They build floats."

Manny nudged Daniel and gave him a thumbs-up sign. "Don't worry, son. Tomorrow, all will be done."

Chapter 1

Daniel hadn't known what he was getting himself into when he suggested he and Logan sponsor floats in the Rose Parade. He'd thought it would be a simple procedure and the magic would happen on its own. But it was one decision after another. How long did he want the float to be? How high? What colors? Which theme? Who, what, where, when, why and how had turned into dozens of meetings despite hiring a company that specialized in float design. Most of his on-air life was taken care of for him. But the decision to sponsor a float had absorbed his off-screen life.

And now, ten months later, the final product was on the verge of emerging.

He sat on a chair in the interview area of the set, about to unveil the design to his viewing audience.

The last six weeks had been the most intense, and now Courtland Float Designs had sent a representative to his show who would be giving weekly updates leading up to the parade.

"My special guest today," Daniel said, "is Miss Greer Courtland." He'd met her father for their initial meetings, but he hadn't met the woman who'd actually designed the float. He stood and clapped his hands.

The pretty woman appeared on the edge of the stage, looking a little nervous. She smiled at him, and he beckoned her forward. She walked across the set almost daintily.

Greer Courtland was a petite woman, maybe five foot four, with pixie-cut hair. She wore a beige silk sheath that clung to her beautiful curves. Daniel couldn't help the immediate attraction he felt to her. Her skin was a lovely, warm nutmeg. Dark brown eyes, almost black, dominated her oval face. Her lips were full and inviting. Too inviting. Daniel could hardly look away from her. She was, in a word, exquisite.

"Welcome to my show," Daniel said, waiting for her to sit.

She perched on the edge of the chair for a second before sliding back and crossing her long, slender legs. "Thank you for inviting me." Her voice was low and sensual.

"So, you designed the float." He held up the final drawing showing his choice. The float consisted of a caterpillar, then a chrysalis and finally several full monarch butterflies at the rear to indicate the year's theme, A Celebration of Life.

She nodded. "I basically work on the engineering to make sure everything runs, twirls and swirls properly and nothing breaks down on Colorado Boulevard."

The audience laughed in approval.

"Let's talk a little about you." He glanced down at the notecards on the small table between them. "You have a degree in structural engineering from Cal Poly Pomona, and you've been designing floats since you were…sixteen." Now, that was impressive. Smart as well as beautiful. He liked that.

"My parents started Courtland Float Designs when I was six years old, and they built it up into what it is today."

"I'm totally fascinated by your family business. You have made a business out of designing floats for the Rose Parade." He felt nothing but awe for her and her family. Who knew anyone could make a business out of parade floats?

"Not just the Rose Parade," Greer said, leaning forward a bit. "We've designed floats for the Macy's Thanksgiving Day Parade, Mardi Gras in New Orleans and Carnival in Rio."

"You've been to Rio. Tell me about Rio."

She grinned coyly at him. "Sorry, no can do. What happens in Rio stays in Rio."

Oh, he had to get the answer to that question. He'd been to Rio a time or two himself. "I'm disappointed you won't share."

Her grin widened. "Rules are rules."

He was very captivated by her. He leaned forward and caught a faint scent of her perfume—a warm vanilla musk with an underlying note of lemon. "I understand you were a Rose Queen."

"Yes, during my senior year in high school. I had a great time that year."

"A Cal Poly graduate *and* a Rose Queen. You're smart and beautiful. What was the hardest part of being the Rose Queen?"

"Number one on the list was how not to look cold. You could be cold, but you could not look like it. Number two was the wave." She held up her hand and started doing the wave.

"You look like the Queen of England."

"We had classes. The wave is sort of like screwing in a lightbulb."

She had the best dimple right next to her mouth when she smiled. The dimple transformed her face, and his gaze was drawn to it. He had a sudden urge to lick that dimple and kiss it. He shook it off and focused on his interview. "What is the hardest part of building a float?"

"Designing something that works and is still beautiful within the boundaries of the rules and regulations of the parade. There's a lot to balance with a float. You have to consider the weight, height and length. The only thing that stays the same every year is the route. You know where all the turns are." Her hands fluttered as she talked, echoing her excitement and passion.

A woman with passion. He could work with that. "I can see you love what you do."

"I get to play in fantasyland all year long, so why not?" Her words came out as a sigh.

"Let's talk a bit about the first step toward getting a float into the parade." When he'd first decided to sponsor a float, he'd had a sharp learning curve.

She sat back, her face taking on a serious look. "The theme for the next year is announced the day after the parade. Once you have the theme, the first step is to create a design. Each designer submits to the parade committee two designs for each float they are commissioned to create. Once the design is approved, we move on to materials and construction."

"Sounds nerve-racking," Daniel said.

She nodded. "You'd think that after making floats for so many years, it would be easy, but it's not. It's like a first date over and over again. You just want to make sure you do everything right and be your best. And hope your underslip doesn't show."

The audience roared with laughter.

Daniel nodded in agreement. He understood being the best. At a signal from the director, he wrapped up this week's interview. "Thank you, Miss Courtland." He turned to the camera. "We'll take a commercial break, and when we come back—weather and traffic." The camera went dark and Daniel stood.

Greer stood with him. "Is it true you and your friend Logan Pierce have a bet on who is going to win the Sweepstakes Trophy?"

"Yes."

"Oh."

"You sound disappointed. A little friendly competition never hurts anyone. You compete with all the other floats."

"I compete with myself. I have seven designs in the parade this year."

Was that disappointing? It almost felt like she was cheating on him before the first date. Because if he had anything to say about it, there would be a date.

"I don't know what to say. I've never had to share a woman before. It feels like you're cheating on me."

She burst into laughter. "Are you serious?"

"I am. I thought I was your one and only."

"No." She shook her head. "My babies have to eat."

The audience roared with laughter. Daniel waved at them. "You have children." She was married! Darn. He hadn't seen that coming.

"Yes."

"Are you married?"

"No."

"I'm a little confused here."

"No, my children are the four-legged kind. Though one of them has only three legs. I designed a float for the Humane Society a couple of years ago and couldn't resist adopting them."

Suddenly he realized she was teasing him. "I'm a dog person."

"I have two dogs and a cat. I'm always looking to add to the family."

His mother would love her. She was smart, beautiful and kind.

"Do you cook?"

She frowned. "What does that have to do with float design?"

"Just some personal information."

"I like to cook, but I don't always have time."

He knew that feeling. If not for his parents occasionally stocking his freezer, he'd have been eating takeout every night of the week. Now in their second careers, his parents owned a restaurant, so the food was always good.

"Well, thank you for coming today. I think the audience loved it," he said. "I look forward to seeing you next week and hearing your report."

"I'll be here."

He walked her off the set just as the camera came live again, but it was pointed at Jennifer, the meteorologist. He didn't have to be back to his desk for another four minutes, and for some reason, he wanted to spend those minutes just watching Greer Courtland walk down the hall.

He waved, and an intern came to escort her out.

Once she was out of sight, he turned back to his desk to get ready for his next segment. But her sexy scent remained in his head for the rest of his day. As did the sound of her husky laughter.

As Greer drove back to her office, she couldn't keep her mind off her handsome host. Daniel Torres was not what she'd expected.

She hadn't wanted to go on his show, but her parents had appointed her. She had been so nervous she feared she'd stutter her way through the segment. She didn't want to embarrass her family, but that sexy hunk of man threw her for a bit of a loop. Never a fan of the unexpected, she almost turned into a puddle of silence when she'd laid eyes on him in person.

As she walked into her office, her sister Rachel peeked in at her and grinned. "We watched the show. You did great. Mom was really impressed."

Greer shrugged. "I tried."

"Is he as handsome in person as he is on the screen?"

"You mean Daniel Torres?" She fanned her face. "Oh yes, he is." She had to admit she liked what she'd seen. "He certainly seemed interested in his float." Though she was a little confused by this competition with his friend. Not that she wasn't a competitive person. She'd had to be at Cal Poly. But this contest had so many random factors. What would happen if neither one took the Sweepstakes Trophy? Or if each won a trophy in a different category? The logistics made her head spin. She was always good about designing floats that could take different trophies. She liked to win, and trophies equaled money in the bank. The float business might have been about making pretty things, but she had to make pretty things that won the shinies.

"Interested in his float? I think he was more interested in you," Rachel said with a sly smile.

A girl could hope. "Don't be absurd. You read the tabloids. That man goes through starlets like they're candy."

"I don't know. If he was in love with any of the starlets, don't you think he'd have gotten married by now?"

"Look at George Clooney. He played the field for decades. Daniel Torres has twenty years to go before he finds his forever wife."

Rachel laughed. "You don't have a romantic bone in your body."

Greer shook her head. "I save all my romance for my floats."

"Yes, and I'm sure they keep you very warm at night."

"Scooter, Pip and Roscoe are very good at keeping my feet warm at night." She didn't need a man. In fact, she didn't think she wanted one on a permanent basis.

"By the way, Chelsea wants you to come over to the warehouse," Rachel told her. "She's testing the hydraulics on Daniel's float."

"I'm on my way."

The warehouse, where the floats were built before being moved to the parking lot of the Rose Bowl for final prep the week before the parade, was a block away from Greer's office in an industrial park. Her sister Chelsea stood next to Daniel's float, a clipboard in hand.

The design presented some height challenges. Floats had to fit underneath the seventeen-foot-high Sierra Madre/I-210 freeway overpass. Anything higher than that had to be lowered by hydraulics in mere seconds. Daniel's final design featured several monarch butterflies flying high off into the sky.

"Good, you're here," Chelsea said.

The skeleton of the float looked eerie without any of the flowers that would be added the final week before the parade. It was all welded steel and covered in chicken wire and plastic.

Other similarly staged floats surrounded Daniel's. A welder sat on the chassis of the adjacent one, his welder spitting fire.

"I enjoyed the show this morning," Chelsea said.

"I wanted Mom and Dad to send you." Greer thought Chelsea was the most beautiful of all of them. She was tall and willowy with a dancer's grace, though at the moment she just looked tired. Her long hair had been pulled into a scrunchie, but half of it was out and floated around her head like a halo.

"I'm too busy." Chelsea handled quality control. Her job was to make sure everything worked right and looked right, down to the smallest detail. "You're in the consulting phase now and can be spared."

"All I have left is to start gluing on flowers." And other organic material. Though flowers were the main starting point for any float, many areas were covered in seeds and grasses to add texture to the overall design.

"I was checking the hydraulics," Chelsea continued, "and I wanted you to watch." She waved at a man half-hidden in a well in the chassis. He waved back, and slowly the butterflies on the rear of the float began to descend.

Before she could comment, Greer's phone rang. "Hello?"

"Miss Greer Courtland? My name is Logan Pierce."

"Excuse me," Greer said, having a hard time hearing over the noise of the welder. She stepped toward the back door open to the parking lot.

"This is Logan Pierce," he repeated. "I saw you on Daniel's show this morning. I was wondering if we could meet."

"Why?" His own float was being built by another company.

"I've never had a woman ask me why I wanted to take her out to dinner."

"I'm asking." She tried to keep the suspicion out of her voice.

"I watched your interview with Daniel, and you were pretty funny. I want to get to know you."

She paused. "How did you get my phone number?" She never gave it to people she didn't know.

"My connections are staggering," he responded with a wry chuckle.

"Really. How did you get my number?"

She could hear the smile in his voice. "I have a personal assistant who would make the CIA, FBI and NSA weep with envy."

"I see." Should she meet with him? She was deeply curious about the rivalry between the two men, and Daniel's answers this morning hadn't satisfied her curiosity. Maybe Logan's would. "I thought you were in New York."

"I'm visiting family for Thanksgiving. My parents still live in Santa Monica."

Meeting him wouldn't hurt, she supposed. "Where do you want to meet?"

"How about dinner at Craig's? I'll pick you up, say around 6:30."

He sounded pleasant enough, but since he was based in New York, she didn't know anything about Logan Pierce.

"No. I'll meet you there." She wasn't about to put herself in a spot she couldn't get out of.

"I'll send a car for you."

"I'll drive myself." She didn't want to be dependent on this man when she didn't know him from Adam. If she wanted to leave, she wanted to be able to do so on her terms.

He laughed, a rich, vibrant sound. "Seven, then, at Craig's."

"Okay," she said before she ended the call. Craig's! That was pretty classy. Celebrities were routinely spotted there, she thought as she turned to find Chelsea watching her. "You'll never guess who that was."

"Daniel Torres asking you out to dinner."

"Close. His friend and float competitor, Logan Pierce."

Chelsea's eyebrows rose. "You're kidding."

"No. I'm meeting him at Craig's tonight."

Chelsea's eyes went wide. "That's the new *in* place."

"You watch too much *TMZ*."

Chelsea punched Greer on the arm. "This is so

exciting. You'd better bring home a doggie bag. For me, not the dog."

She laughed. "I'll try to remember."

After giving her approval on the hydraulics, Greer headed back to her office, till her father stopped her in the hallway.

"Meeting." Roman Courtland was a man of few words.

She followed him into his large corner office overlooking the industrial park. Every available inch of wall space was covered with photos of the award-winning floats by Courtland Floats Designs, along with family photos.

Her mother stood at the window, a bottle of water in one hand. Tall and slim, Virginia Courtland wore a cream-colored pantsuit with a colorful Hermes scarf about her neck. She'd styled her black hair into a sleek French roll that emphasized her sharply defined cheekbones. She'd been born in Los Angeles after her parents had migrated from Bermuda nearly sixty years ago. Virginia's father had been an actor with minor parts in nearly a hundred films. He'd made a good living but never attained a higher status than character actor.

Greer's father, Roman, was of medium height with a thick head of curly black hair threaded with gray. He wore jeans and a black sweater with the sleeves pushed up. Like Virginia, he was LA-born, but his family had been in Los Angeles since the early 1800s. His ancestors had managed to escape from slavery in Georgia and thought to make a place for themselves in Spanish-held California. His two-times great-grandfather had been Native American, and the Nez Perce heritage showed in his slightly hooked nose and wide-spaced eyes.

Roman looked tired. These last few weeks before the parade were the most intense and stressful. All the labor of the last ten months culminated in round-the-clock shifts as floats were checked for any last-minute issues before heading to the staging tent set up on the Rose Bowl parking lot. There, hundreds of volunteers needed to finish the floral decoration on time.

Greer grabbed a bottle of water from the under-counter fridge behind her father's desk and sat down on the sofa. "I think this morning's interview went well."

Her mother nodded as she took a seat in one of the chairs. "He seemed to ask you a lot of personal questions."

"He made me a little uncomfortable."

"You handled yourself well," her father said as he sat in the other chair and crossed one leg over the other.

"Rose Queen training," Greer answered. She took a sip of water.

"I wish he'd allowed you to talk more about the float."

"They want me to come back on a weekly basis now that it's coming down to the wire," Greer said. "They want to do some on-site filming, too. Dad, what were you thinking?'"

Roman gave her an innocent look. "What do you think I'm thinking?"

"Why did you take on a celebrity client? Not that he's been a problem, but now I have to budget a morning to do an interview when I should be overseeing the final decorating."

"You work too hard," he said. "In the last four years, two other companies have popped into the float business. If we want to stay ahead of the game, we need to put ourselves out there. And you are the perfect person to do that. You've got the degree in structural engineering. Not to put down your sisters, but they chose more nonscience degrees."

"Smooth, Dad, smooth."

Chelsea had a degree in Elizabethan literature, and Rachel had a degree in finance.

"Don't get us wrong," her mother interjected, obviously in agreement with her husband. "You all bring something to the table, but you ensure the structural integrity of every float. Without you, the floats might collapse in the middle of the parade. Do not make me remind you of the great float debacle in 2001, which forced your dad to go out on his own."

Greer simply grinned at her mother. "I get it." She slanted a glance at her father. "You told your boss that the float wouldn't work and you were right." The float fell apart a half hour into the two-and-a-half-hour parade and had to be pulled out of line and pushed back to the staging area.

"It was a beautiful day," Roman said with a wide grin.

And being the only African American family in

the float business had brought its own level of notice, letting others know what one family could achieve when they worked together.

"I still think the interview went well," Greer said. "Next time I'll be better prepared and won't let him drag me off topic."

"You were pretty amusing off topic," Virginia said with a chuckle.

"The wave has gone viral," Roman said.

"We need to take you off social media," Greer retorted. She took another sip of her water. "Dad, did Logan Pierce approach you about designing his float?"

"No," Roman said. "He went with Associated Float Design. Why?"

"He called me and wants to meet for dinner tonight."

"Are you going?" Virginia asked.

"Sure. Why not? Maybe I'll get some answers to this rivalry he and Daniel Torres have going." She stood and yawned. Maybe she shouldn't have accepted Logan's dinner invitation. She needed sleep more than good food.

At exactly seven o'clock, Greer pulled to a stop in front of Craig's. The valet opened the door to her Toyota 4Runner and held a hand out for her. She accepted the help. He handed her a ticket and took her keys.

She'd dressed carefully for her meeting with Logan. After going through her closet, she'd chosen a pearl-gray silk sheath with a matching jacket trimmed in black satin ribbon. She wore a silver locket that looked perfect with her gray and stylish silver earrings. Black stilettos and a clutch purse completed her look. She'd smoothed her hair back from her face and kept her makeup at a minimum.

She glanced around as she entered the restaurant. She'd never been to Craig's before. The facade only hinted at the elegance inside. She stepped into the warmth and was immediately greeted by the hostess. "I'm meeting—"

"Mr. Pierce is waiting for you, Miss Courtland," the hostess said smoothly. "If you'll follow me."

Craig's had an elegant feel to it. The walls were dark wainscoting with brick above it. Art hung at intervals on the wall. Brick pillars supported the ceiling. The hostess led Greer to a prominently placed booth. Logan Pierce slid out and stood, a smile spread across his face. He was a muscular man a few inches taller than Greer. She didn't know if his carefully brushed and arranged blond hair was natural or bleached, but he looked good. Sparkling blue eyes met hers and he grinned, showing perfect teeth of a dazzling white.

He held out his hand. "Thank you for coming, Miss Courtland. May I call you Greer?"

She slid into the booth and he sat across from her. "Please, if I can call you Logan."

Logan nodded. The hostess walked away, and a few seconds later, a member of the waitstaff approached. Mona, as she introduced herself, placed glasses of water in front of them and then asked for their drink order.

"Merlot, please," Greer said.

The woman listed the different brands, and Greer chose one. She didn't recognize the label but knew it would be excellent. Craig's would offer nothing less. Logan ordered bourbon on the rocks.

"Thank you for coming," Logan said.

"Why?" she asked. "Why do you want to have dinner with me?"

He looked taken aback for a second but recovered neatly. "I thought you might be hungry."

She laughed. "It is dinnertime, so you didn't make a bad assumption. But I don't think that's your real reason."

"Why do you think I asked you out?" He leaned toward her.

"I assumed you wanted information on Daniel's Rose Parade float."

His eyebrows went up, and his blue eyes sparkled with mischief. "You caught me."

Greer narrowed her eyes. "I didn't think I was your type."

"I like smart, funny women."

The waitress brought their drinks. As Greer took a sip of the excellent wine, a shadow fell across the table, and she glanced up to find Daniel standing in front of them. A tiny, dainty-featured blonde woman hung on his arm. Greer recognized her from her TV show but couldn't remember her name.

"Mind if we join you?" Daniel motioned the actress into the booth next to Logan and then pushed in next to Greer.

As Greer shifted over, she noticed Logan's face. He looked completely surprised, especially when the blonde woman slipped closer to him with a tiny purr. Daniel simply smiled.

"What are you doing here?" Logan asked, his voice sounding choked.

"Got to eat," Daniel replied. "You're my best friend and I thought I'd join you. We don't get to spend much time together."

"You normally take your dates to your parents' restaurant."

"Not tonight," Daniel said cheerfully. "Pass me the bread please, Greer."

Greer pushed the bread basket toward him, shifting a little further away. "You're interrupting my date."

"I'm saving you from boredom. Logan has two subjects—himself and sports."

"I do not," Logan objected.

"You told me last week you wanted to meet Melody Wilkerson. So I called her up and invited her to meet you."

Melody giggled, putting a childlike hand over her mouth. "I've been dying to meet you for years."

Greer sat back and watched as the woman walked her fingers up Logan's arm and pouted prettily. "Why did you bring that woman on my date?" she half whispered to Daniel.

"You shouldn't be dating Logan."

"Why not?" she asked.

"Because you should be dating me." Daniel grinned at her.

"You didn't ask me out."

"I didn't expect Logan to work this fast."

"I see. So you brought Melody as a distraction while you fling me over your shoulder and carry me out."

He laughed. "That wasn't my plan, but I'm terrific at unexpected modifications."

Greer shook her head, trying not to laugh. "You're too funny."

Daniel gave her a cheeky grin. "The only people who think I'm funny are my brothers."

"Oh no, this was funny." She gestured at Melody, who'd totally captured Logan with one hand on his arm and the other touching his hand playfully. She was so tiny, Greer wondered if she bought her clothes in the children's department.

"Look at him," Daniel told her. "He's so easily distracted."

Logan was studying Melody's low-cut top and the perky breasts beneath it.

"I guess those things are mesmerizing. And most likely fake."

Daniel shrugged. "I wouldn't know."

"Really?" Greer glanced back at Melody, who leaned into Logan's arm, brushing her breasts against the sleeve of his jacket.

"Melody isn't my type."

"You brought her."

"I'm just being a good friend." He gave her an innocent, almost angelic look.

"I think you're being diabolical."

He gave her an evil henchman laugh, and she shook her head. Daniel Torres was charming. Too charming. And yet she could see that he'd chosen a good distraction. Logan was falling under Melody's spell.

"You chose your weapon well," she finally said. "Though why you two are dueling over me, I don't know. Let me ask you something. Do you really want to date me, or just win? If my float had feelings, it would feel cheap, used, unappreciated."

He leaned toward her and half whispered in her ear. "Do *you* feel cheap, used and unappreciated?"

"Goodness, no. I'm amused. You're like two kindergarteners fighting over a swing."

"Are you saying I'm a child?"

"Mmm. Let my silence speak volumes." She took a sip of her wine.

"You and I should sneak out of here and get some burgers." Daniel nudged her with his elbow. "Logan won't notice we're gone."

Greer considered his invitation. "No. Logan asked me out to dinner, and to leave now would be extremely rude."

Daniel sulked for a moment. "Okay. My mother did bring me up well."

The waitress brought extra menus and returned a few minutes later to take their food order, patiently answering Melody's questions about nutrition and the number of calories of different dishes.

Dinner turned out to be pleasant enough even though Melody greedily ensnared Logan's attention throughout the meal. He looked embarrassed, but Greer patted his shoulder and told him to enjoy himself. She was enjoying herself watching the two men.

As they stood out on the sidewalk after dinner, Melody clung to Logan like a limpet. The valet brought his Mercedes and Melody climbed in, not even asking if Greer needed a ride home. As the Mercedes sped away, Greer's Toyota came to a stop in front of her. She tipped the valet with a smile and as he held the door open for her, she looked at Daniel.

"If you want to date me, then ask." She slid into her car, put it in gear and left before Daniel could answer.

Chapter 2

Daniel's phone chimed. He glanced at the display. Greer had responded to his text, and he smiled. He'd sent several texts thanking her for an enjoyable dinner and telling her how great the float was going to look. Her dedication to her work showed, and he couldn't have been more pleased.

He'd felt a little sorry for crashing Logan's date. Not sorry enough to stop himself. Greer wasn't for Logan. She was too down-to-earth, too practical. Logan liked winsome, waiflike women who barely looked old enough to vote. Greer would have run circles around him.

The door to his office opened, and his twin entered.

"Hey, bro," Nicholas said with a disarming grin.

They might have been twins, but they were opposites. Nicholas was the creative type. Tall and lean, he'd always liked to dance, and somehow along the way dancing had evolved into choreographing. Any man who considered dance and choreography unmasculine had never met Nicholas. How many men could catch a woman who'd just flung herself into the air and then lift her above him and make it all look as though she was as light as a feather?

"What brings you to my studio?" He set down a stack of papers. Daniel had been working on material for his next show. His special guest would be a rising young actor who was thought to be the next action-adventure hero, and Daniel wanted interview questions that weren't the run-of-the-mill, media-hype questions about his next movie.

"Thought you might be interested in this." He handed Daniel a tabloid magazine. "I'm impressed."

Daniel's photo was prominent on the cover. He stood next to Logan with Melody in between as they left Craig's. The headline Love Triangle was splashed across the top. A tiny bit of Greer's elbow could be seen at one edge.

"Why do you bother reading this stuff?" Daniel shoved the tabloid back at Nicholas.

Nicholas sat down in the leather chair across from Daniel. "Because the fun is in finding the grain of truth inside the speculation."

"These magazines are all about speculation. They throw information at you from undisclosed sources and hope the reader will come to some sort of salacious conclusion." Daniel hated being in the tabloids. Usually he managed to avoid them, but being with Logan the other night had changed that. A few photographers had been dogging Logan the last couple of days, hoping for that one sensational photo that would bring them the big bucks.

"That's the fun," Nicholas said cheerfully. "I know where this night ended up in my head."

"Get your mind out of the gutter, Nicky," Daniel growled. Nicholas hated being called Nicky. But his brother just grinned in delight. "Why are you here?"

"Just needed a chat with my bro."

Daniel eyed his brother. "What do you want?"

"I want be on the float with you."

Daniel was so taken aback he could only stare. "You do? Why?"

"Why not? Me dancing on the float would be great advertising for the next season of *Celebrity Dance*. After all, we're on the same network. I talked to my bosses, and they will be talking to your bosses."

Daniel rubbed his temple. "I guess that means you're going to have to meet with Greer. She has this complex rule about weight and positioning and stuff I would never think about."

"She thinks like a dancer."

"Is that good or bad?"

"In my world that's a good thing," Nicholas replied. "Explain what happened to you and Logan." He tapped the magazine.

"I crashed Logan's date with Greer and I took Melody along to distract him."

"And you did this why?"

"I didn't want him going out with Greer." He sounded childish even to himself.

"You're not five years old anymore, bro." Nicholas shook his head.

"He's just not her type," Daniel objected.

"And you are?"

"Of course I am. Or at least, I'd like to be." Daniel realized he deeply admired her. "She's fascinating. She was a Rose Queen." He remembered her teasing wave.

"That's not the only reason you're interested in her." Nicholas eyed Daniel with a sparkle in his dark brown eyes.

"Something about her is real. She's smart and funny, and I've always liked smart and funny. Who knew a person could make a living designing and building floats? They're beautiful."

Nicholas shrugged. "She's certainly different from the normal actress/model/singer you ordinarily date."

"Why are we talking about girls?" Usually Daniel and his brother talked about everything, but for some reason Daniel was reluctant to talk about Greer.

"We talk about girls all the time," Nicholas said with a short laugh. "You're just uncomfortable, and I'm enjoying it."

Daniel ignored the comment and focused on the real reason for his brother's visit. "Like I said, you're going to need to talk to Greer, because I don't know how you're going to dance with the butterfly."

"I'm dancing with the butterfly, all right. I'm bringing Michelle Mercer."

Michelle was one of the other professional dancers on Nicholas's show. They had danced together before when Nicholas had first started out and landed in a Broadway show. Daniel had met her once and thought she was nice enough, but a bit flighty.

"I'll set up an appointment, and we'll head over to the warehouse where Greer works." Daniel made a note to himself to call her later.

Nicholas let himself out with a small wave and a thank-you.

Daniel sat back in his chair, wondering why he liked Greer so much. Most of the women he dated were beautiful models, or actresses, or in the industry. He dated them to be seen. He saw them as stepping stones for his career. But Greer was different. Different in a way that he liked.

He wanted to explore his feelings more, but a ton of work awaited him on his desk, and he needed to get back to it.

Greer stood to the side of the skeleton that would be Daniel's float. The caterpillar was a long piece of plastic tubing, articulated in a dozen sections. The head would move back and forth on its own little motor. The chrysalis hung from a tangle of wire shaped into a branch. And three butterflies flew out the rear of the float. As Chelsea operated the hydraulics, the wings moved in a stately flight pattern, and the butterflies went up and down.

Greer had to figure out where to place the two additional bodies Daniel had told her about. She tried not to be irritated, especially because Daniel had told her that the studio wanted to hire her to design their annual Hollywood Christmas parade float. The lucrative offer tempered her irritation.

"Where are you putting the two other people?" Chelsea asked as she jumped down off the chassis.

"I think if we move the caterpillar back a foot, there's room to put a small dance floor," Greer replied. "It'll be cramped but doable. And Daniel's brother is a professional dancer. I'm sure he'll know how work in that small a space." Daniel had his spot to one side of the driver, and one of his coworkers would occupy the other side. He told her he hadn't decided yet who that would be.

"I've watched *Celebrity Dance*, and I have to admit, he's all kinds of yummy," Chelsea said. "Are you okay with him being all kinds of yummy?"

"A girl has to be flexible."

"I remember the great axle disaster of 2010." Chelsea laughed and picked up her clipboard from where she'd placed it before crawling onto the float.

"We were all being flexible that year. Who knew we could tear a float down and put it back together in four days on a completely different chassis?" Greer had just about torn her hair out because the new chassis had been slighter higher and longer, which meant extra surface, more flowers for coverage and a rebalancing of the weight.

Greer shrugged. "I guess after that challenge, this is a piece of cake."

"I knew you'd say that." Chelsea had moved to the next float and jumped up on the chassis. Trident Airlines was a longtime customer, and every year their float won a trophy. This year their float was unusually intricate and long. It was actually two flatbeds in length, and getting it around corners had been a problem Greer had eventually solved by installing clamps in the center that could be loosened enough to make the float flexible in the center and then reattached once it was straight again.

"I think I've finalized the flower order," Chelsea said as she walked back to Greer. "Can you look it over and make sure I didn't forget anything?"

"Here's hoping a Kodiak bear doesn't hiccup in Alaska and cause a tsunami somewhere and wipe out the flower harvest."

"Think good thoughts, girl. If we get into trouble, we'll do a commando raid on Mrs. Allenworth's greenhouse. Her orchids are looking spectacular this year. And her roses are so beautiful, I have to pinch myself to keep from stealing some."

"You criminal you," Greer said with a laugh. "It's a good thing she has that bloodthirsty Chihuahua to keep you a law-abiding citizen." Mrs. Allenworth had been a Rose Queen in the sixties and now donated flowers. Chelsea spread them out over all their floats as a way to honor the elderly woman.

Greer followed Chelsea to the next float. A workman on scaffolding bent over the high end of the float with a blowtorch, adding wire to finish the branches on a metal tree. The float represented the Tree of Life, and Greer was delighted with the final look.

"How was your date with Logan-slash-Daniel?" Chelsea asked as she took out her tape measure to reassess an area that would be covered in grass. She was big about measuring everything twice. "I saw the tabloid with Logan, Daniel and that actress on the cover. How did this love triangle happen?"

Greer just shrugged, pretending to be busy.

"Weren't you there?" her sister prompted.

"I was there," she replied with a little sigh, resigned to discuss the evening. "Daniel turned up about ten minutes into my meeting with Logan—by the way, it wasn't a date—with this Melody on his arm. Before I knew it, he'd deposited her on Logan, and he was sitting with me. I'm not quite sure how he managed it. That man is smooth."

"Sounds like he's wooing you."

"Why?" Greer asked. "I'm not sure I'm worth wooing. I don't have time for romance."

"Yeah, I know. Your last date was two years ago." Chelsea rolled up her tape measure, tucked it back in her pocket and wrote on her clipboard. "Where do you want your life to go?"

"I want to design floats and grow the business."

"I mean your personal life."

Greer leaned against a float. "You're the one getting a divorce."

"Which just proves I'm at least out having a life. I may be making bad choices, but I'm trying."

"My little glass-is-half-full sister. What would I do without your boundless enthusiasm?"

Chelsea crossed her arms over her chest. "Mom received tickets to the preview of Henry Ossawa Tanner's show, and I know she and Dad can't make it. She'll give them to you if you ask nicely. Why not call Daniel and ask him to go with you?"

"You're kidding me."

Chelsea shook her head. "I never kid about men. Men are no joke."

Chelsea should know. Her husband, a research biologist with the California Department of Fish and Wildlife, took life very seriously, as well as all the cute little interns who came along to help him count bunnies. Chelsea hadn't made a bad choice. She'd had a lot in common with her soon-to-be ex-husband. He was the one who couldn't keep his hands to himself.

"And that could be our problem," Greer said. "We don't laugh enough about men."

"Are you going to call Daniel?"

Greer didn't know if she had the guts to call him. She liked what she knew about him but…did she want to take a risk? She took risks at work, but she liked to play her personal life safe. It was easier that way. "I'll think about it."

"Okay, I'll accept that. Let's get back to work. This flower order isn't going to get itself done." Chelsea moved on to the next float, Greer following in her wake.

* * *

It was hours later when Greer headed back to her office.

"You have a visitor," her sister Rachel called out as Greer passed her open door.

Greer stuck her head in her sister's office. It was piled high with files, bankers' boxes and assorted supplies. Her sister, the company accountant, looked frazzled, her hair frizzing around her face like a halo. At twenty-five, Rachel was the youngest of the three sisters and also the most logical. Like the other Courtlands, she was an extremely hard worker.

"Who is it?" Greer asked.

"You're new bestie, Daniel Torres." Rachel turned back to her computer, her fingers flying over the keys.

Greer made her way down the hall. She loved her office. Her parents had given her carte blanche in decorating it. She'd chosen a red leather sofa and two floral wingback chairs flanking an oak coffee table. Her desk was a slanted artist's table facing away from the huge window that overlooked the parking lot. A rolling chest sat next to it containing her art supplies. She'd painted the walls bright white and then hung drawings of her prize-winning floats along with her diploma from Cal Poly Pomona.

Daniel stood in front of a painting of a float that had won her a first-place ribbon in an art show her senior year in high school. He turned to her as she stepped in. "You're very talented."

"Thank you. What are you doing here?" Greer asked.

"Your sister Chelsea called me to go over the final flower order, and I thought I'd stop in and say hi to you." He strolled around her office, pausing briefly in front of each drawing.

She couldn't decide if she was irritated or flattered. "That's nice. Chelsea is in the warehouse."

"I'll get to her." As if waving her off, he continued to gaze at the drawings. "With all this talent, why did you go into structural engineering?"

"I wanted to make magic."

"And you do." He pointed at a drawing of a jaguar that looked as though it were about to leap. "I really like this one."

"That's the float I did for Carnival in Rio this year. I like it, too." Since he didn't seem to be in a hurry to leave, she politely asked, "Would you like some coffee, water, tea?"

"Nothing, thank you." He gestured at her drawings. "This is magic for you?"

"I get the chance to create something that is enjoyed for a day. It's a challenge. Besides that, I get to hang with the coolest people in the world—my family."

"I understand. I like my family, too."

"Did you really intend to sabotage my meeting with Logan by showing up with Melody?" she asked him bluntly. No one would accuse her of subtlety.

His eyebrows rose in surprise. "Logan was hoping the meeting would turn into a date, but another shiny girl came along and he got confused."

Greer's eyes narrowed. "With a lot of help from you."

"What are friends for?" He kept grinning at her as though he'd pulled something over on her, too.

She didn't know whether to be irritated, amused or flattered. "Since you're here, I'm wondering if you'd like to attend the preview party on Saturday at the Norton Simon Museum for Henry Ossawa Tanner. I have tickets." That really came out of her mouth? *Oh, Greer, you silly girl.*

"Are you asking me out on a date?"

"Sure, we'll call it a date. But…I have some rules. No Melody. No other starlet. No Logan hijacking me. And do you think we can ditch the paparazzi? I managed to avoid being a part of that love-triangle story, and I don't want to see my face on a tabloid."

He looked like a kid who'd just been handed the best present ever. "I can manage that. It's not like I'm Kanye, or Madonna, or Beyoncé. The paparazzi don't really follow me around hoping to snap a photo of me doing something disgraceful."

"Done."

"Are you going to let me pick you up, or do you want to meet at the museum?"

She paused, thinking. "On a first date, I like to have my own escape route if something doesn't go well."

"Technically, it's our second date."

He looked so hopeful, she didn't have the heart to decline. And he was sort of right. She conceded to him on this. "Pick me up at seven. I'll text you my address."

Chelsea poked her head into Greer's office and grinned at Daniel. "Good, you're here. I want to go over some things with you for final approval."

With a quick goodbye and a dazzling smile, Daniel followed Chelsea down the hall, leaving Greer to think about what she'd just done. She had asked him out on a date! But she had to admit it—Daniel had something about him that she just liked. She couldn't quite put her finger on it. He was charming and good-looking and had an interesting sense of humor. His baiting of Logan at their dinner had been fun in a very odd way. Bottom line: she wanted to know more about the man who was Daniel Torres.

The gym smelled of damp clothes, overheated bodies and good, honest man-sweat. Daniel had finished his workout. Logan sat next to him on a bench as they watched the people around them. Several women on treadmills competed with two men who had revved their treadmills up to the fastest setting and were running frantically while the women pretended to ignore them. A bank of windows on one side of the gym showed a class of women doing yoga. Two personal trainers coached their clients, and a cute woman with a truly buff body was spotting on a bench press for her own client.

"She asked you out!" Logan stared at Daniel.

"Who doesn't want to date this package?" Daniel teased.

"I don't," Logan said with a snicker.

"You have no taste."

"I have great taste…in women." Logan wiped his sweaty face with his towel. "And Greer is all woman."

"She is beautiful, but she wasn't beautiful enough to keep you from ogling Melody."

Logan sighed. "I'm going to have to find a way to make that up to her."

"Let it lie. Let her be angry with you for the rest of your life."

Logan gave him a piercing look. "You like her. You like her a lot."

Daniel saw the challenge in Logan's eyes. "We've never sparred over a woman before."

"That's because I've always won the ones I wanted." Logan's face took on a dreamy look.

"Or one could say I allowed you to win the ones I wanted you to have."

Logan burst out laughing. "This never gets old, does it?"

Daniel smiled. "I'm going to be your friend for-ever."

Daniel had met Logan during their freshman year of high school on the football team. Logan had been the quarterback and Daniel the wide receiver. They both had loved football, but Logan had wanted to make a career out of it while Daniel just wanted to play the game.

Logan's home life hadn't been the best. His parents had never been around. His father, a talent agent, traveled a lot, and his mother, a character actress, was always on the set of some movie. Logan had been raised mostly by nannies. The first time Daniel brought him home, his parents had taken the boy under their wing and made sure that this spoiled little rich kid act turned into a responsible adult.

In their first encounter, Logan made a pass but had stepped out of bounds, and no one noticed. Daniel caught the pass, made the touchdown and got the win, but Daniel had called Logan to task for his maneuver.

Logan had been amazed that Daniel cared. Daniel had talked to him about fairness and doing the right thing. Doing the right thing had intrigued Logan because his parents hadn't had that level of ethics. Daniel's parents, on the other hand, were all about being ethical and insisted Logan fall into step with them if he wanted to be Daniel's friend. Because Logan did want to be Daniel's friend, he'd allowed Grace and Manny Torres to mold him. He'd once told Daniel that he liked the Torres family rules because he knew exactly what was expected of him.

"I'm not going to stop chasing after her," Logan said after a long silence. "If you think she's that intriguing, then she must be, and you know how I like to be intrigued."

They lifted their water bottles and clunked them together. "Good luck with that. As much as you like being intrigued, you are easily distracted."

Logan gave Daniel a look. "Wait a minute. Are you saying you aren't playing fair?"

"The better man is going to win." Daniel knew he sounded arrogant, but he really liked Greer. His

mother would like her, and Grace didn't give her approval easily. She expected her children to act with
the highest standards and to find partners who would
do the same thing.

What was he thinking? Why was he even putting
the words *marriage* and *Greer* in the same thought?

Greer stood in front of the full-length mirror in her
bedroom. She'd tried on five cocktail dresses in the
hope of finding just the right one. She finally chose
her Anna Sui black-and-yellow-daisy cocktail dress
with black lace inserts on the bodice. She brushed
her short hair straight back from her face and added
diamond drop earrings and a matching pendant on a
gold chain. She was as ready as she would ever be.

She grabbed her black silk clutch, took a deep
breath and walked out to the living room to wait for
Daniel. She sat in a chair in front of the huge living
room window.

She'd saved for five years to purchase her tiny
Craftsman bungalow. The bungalow had been a fixer-
upper. Though she didn't have the skills to renovate
the house for herself, she did know people. Half the
float staff at the warehouse had pitched in and helped
her, and she was proud of the results.

She'd decorated with Stickley furniture she'd gotten on sale at a local furniture store and hung her own
vividly colored paintings on the walls. Oriental rugs
covered the polished wood floors, and reproduction
Tiffany lamps sat on tables, adding the vintage look
she'd wanted.

When she saw a limo pull into her driveway, she stood, surprised. She hadn't expected Daniel to rent a limo for the night, though she had to admit going to Norton Simon seemed like a limo-worthy affair.

Daniel stepped out of the limo and walked up the garden path to her front porch. A second later the doorbell rang. In the kitchen, her dogs barked. Her cat lifted her tiny black head, blinking in annoyance at the interruption to her nap.

Greer opened the front door and saw Daniel's eyes widen in surprise as he dragged his eyes down her body from head to toe.

"Wow!" was all he said.

"I clean up nice, don't I?" she teased. "You do, too." He looked so handsome in his black suit.

He must have heard the dogs scratching the kitchen door, because he looked beyond her. "Your dogs, I guess?"

She nodded. "They're in the kitchen and no doubt itching to get out and smell their guest."

"Then let's meet them."

She opened the door to the kitchen. Two medium-sized white-and-tan dogs jumped out, their claws clicking on the wood floor. They sniffed Daniel's shoes and legs and then looked up at him with their appealing brown eyes.

"This is Roscoe and this is Pip. Who could resist them?" She knelt down and ruffled their ears.

The cat jumped down from the chair she'd been sleeping in and walked over. "That's Scooter. She had a litter of kittens that died, and she ended up adopting Roscoe and Pip as newborn puppies when their mother rejected them. It seemed sad to separate them. I'm kind of weak that way."

When the dogs were satisfied Daniel wasn't a threat, they went back into the kitchen and out the doggie door. Scooter returned to her chair and her nap.

"Shall we get going?" Daniel asked.

Greer grabbed her clutch and a black silk shawl. Even though the evening was fairly mild, a slight chill hung in the air when Daniel opened the front door.

"This is nice," she said once they were settled in the backseat of the limo.

"I'm excited about the exhibit. I've admired Henry Ossawa Tanner since I first discovered him when I took an art class. How did you score the tickets?"

"My parents have always supported the arts and have been members of the museum for over twenty years. I'm keeping up the tradition."

Daniel poured her a glass from a bottle of crisp chardonnay cooling in a bucket of ice. She accepted it and settled back to enjoy the ride. He motioned toward a tray of canapés on a tiny table that pulled out from the side. She sampled a couple.

"So tell me," she said after another sip of wine. "Is there a possibility that Logan will show up tonight with your dream date?"

He laughed. "I doubt it. Logan's idea of art is the *Sports Illustrated* swimsuit edition."

"I wonder what he would say about your idea of art."

"I'm a big fan of impressionism and postmodernism. Before they opened their restaurant, my parents were performers, and my siblings and I were exposed to down-on-their-luck writers and artists all the time. They fed a lot of them. My mother has a soft spot for anyone who needs a good meal. My dad grew up poor and black in Brazil, where there wasn't a lot of food. If you're hungry, he'll feed you."

"I've met your parents," Greer said. His mother had so much energy she made other people look like they were standing still. "I designed a float for the North Hollywood Businessmen's Association a couple of years ago. And I designed a float for Carnival in Rio last year that your mom commissioned." That float had been a lot of fun and had also been the most elaborate one she'd ever designed. Rio was deadly serious about their Mardi Gras celebration.

They spoke awhile about her work on those jobs. Then she couldn't help asking the question that had been burning in her brain. "Why did you accept my invitation? Were you trying to make Logan jealous?"

"I'm a man," he said with a grin. "Of course I wanted to make Logan jealous, but that isn't the number one reason."

"Before we get to the number one reason, what number was that on your list?"

He thought for a moment, and Greer was amused at the tiny frown that appeared between his eyes. "Number six."

"And number one is…"

He studied her. "You're the most intriguing woman

I've met in years. You're like a mystery I want to un-ravel. You were a Rose Queen, and that beats a prom queen or homecoming queen any day. And you de-sign the most beautiful floats."

She smiled and inclined her head. Her year as Rose Queen had been filled with events that had kept her busy and on display. She'd loved every minute of it, even though her duties took her away from her fam-ily for days at a time.

The limo pulled up to the museum's main entrance and waited behind a line of cars dropping people off. When they finally pulled up to the dropoff spot, Dan-iel jumped out of the car and helped her out. She draped her shawl around her shoulders, and as they walked up the stairs, he tucked her hand around his arm.

The Norton Simon Museum was alive with light, laughter and music. People congregated in groups as they walked inside. Chamber music came from a three-piece orchestra situated in a corner of the foyer.

Greer loved the museum. As a child, her parents had brought her and her sisters to workshops designed to introduce children to the arts and even allow them to try their hand at painting and sculpting. She'd taken her first art class at the age of six. Her talent had stood out so strongly that her parents started bringing her for art classes every Saturday.

"Greer Courtland," a voice called out.

Greer turned to find Patricia Galen waving at her. "Patty."

"I'd hoped you'd come tonight." Patty was a tall,

slim woman in her midforties. She scheduled many of the art events for the children's workshops. "When can you teach another class on float design and engineering? I receive requests for you all the time. Your workshop has always been one of the more popular ones."

"Not until after Mardi Gras. I fly down to Rio in mid-January with my sister to oversee the last stages of the float we have there," Greer said. "I'll be back the day after the celebration. March and April are my down times."

"How about something for late March?" Patty consulted her iPhone. "I have an opening on the third Saturday."

"I can do that. I'll call you next week and we can plan it out."

Patty smiled at Daniel, but before Greer could introduce him, she'd flitted off to talk to someone else.

"You teach?" Daniel asked her.

She detected admiration in his voice. That meant he was impressed on an intellectual level, which made her feel a little tingly. And she liked it. "I dabble more than I teach."

"You're an interesting woman, Greer Courtland."

She smiled. "Isn't that your number one reason for accepting my invitation to this event?"

He gave her a salacious grin. "Yeah, I'm going with that."

That made her laugh and feel comfortable all at the same time. Daniel Torres was a dangerous man… in a good way.

The entry doors stood open. Members of the board of trustees stood at the doors, greeting people. Greer shook hands with them as they passed.

Once inside, Greer and Daniel followed the line to the exhibition hall.

"So why did you ask me to come with you?" Daniel asked when they stopped at the door. An attendant handed them a booklet describing the paintings that waited for them inside.

"Do I have to have a reason?"

"I have one."

She shook her head. "I didn't think you'd be interested in art. Consider this a test."

He glanced at her. There was a glint of disbelief in his eyes. "A test? A test of what?"

"To see if you're interested in things that interest me." Most men she met weren't. They got only one date. Daniel, she was sure, was heading to date number two with no problem.

"Did I pass?"

Was it her or did he look a little worried? Oh, how sweet. She loved that his ego didn't get in the way. Well, at least not a lot. "Yes. I can see you're just as excited to be here tonight as I am. So you pass."

"Do I get an A?"

"Don't press your luck. This is only the first week of school."

He grinned at her. He rested his hand on her back as they entered the exhibit hall. His touch felt right. Not too brazen. Respectful yet sexy. The place where his hand touched warmed and prickled. She didn't even think about moving away from him. In fact, she had to fight the urge to move closer.

People wandered around the room, stopping to study the paintings hanging on the walls.

"Do you have a favorite?" Daniel asked as they strolled.

"*View of the Seine*, though I don't think it's here." She flipped through the booklet and discovered she was correct. Though the museum had scored *The Banjo Lesson*, Tanner's most famous. Greer's parents had taught her to be proud of her heritage. She liked the idea that she was creating her own legacy. She often marveled that her parents had lived through some turbulent times when African American culture was treated with disdain, yet they'd kept their pride intact. "Do you have a favorite?"

"I have to admit, I don't know very much about him personally, but I do like his work." Daniel paused to study a Biblical painting.

"Then let me share the knowledge I picked up as a junior docent here."

"Rose Queen and a docent at a prestigious art museum. I'm impressed."

She chuckled. "Tanner was influential and is considered the best African American painter. He even got his own postage stamp." She flipped through the booklet to show Daniel the stamp.

"Only the best of the best get a stamp." He stepped back as though studying her. "I'm having a hard time picturing you as a docent."

"Working as a docent was an incredible life lesson. I learned everything I could about art and how to deal with strangers and talk to anybody. Pasadena is a very close-knit community. Everybody knows everybody."

"I noticed," he said. "Seven people have nodded to you already."

"Are you sure they're not looking at you?"

"No. You're the beauty here. And I'm enjoying being ignored."

"I always thought people in your business liked being noticed."

"I like being noticed when I want to be noticed."

"So it's all about what you want."

"You were in any doubt?"

She tucked her hand through his arm and leaned into him. "God forbid I should have a moment of doubt."

She led him to the next painting, *Sodom and Gomorrah*. This was another favorite of hers. She loved the rich colors of the billowing smoke as Lot and his family fled the doomed cities. The pillar of salt that had been Lot's wife looked sad and lonely.

Eventually they made their way to the sculpture garden, her favorite place in the whole museum. They found a small secluded area and sat on a bench.

"Thank you for inviting me," Daniel said.

She liked the sincerity in his voice. She had thought he would be a bit blasé about coming. Art exhibits were pretty tame events compared to what he was probably used to. The fact that he was obviously enjoying himself made her like him more. "I thought you might like it. Though I did wonder. The focus of your morning show is the current movie, or the trending starlet, so I wasn't certain culture was high on your list."

"You have a very sad impression of me," Daniel said. "You know, people thought Henry Ossawa Tanner wasn't an artist because of who he was and where he came from. Aren't you glad they were wrong?"

Good for him that he had no problem challenging her. "Touché," she replied. "I deserved that. I usually judge people by their actions, but you're in the tabloids so often, I have a hard time thinking you are different."

"Ninety-five percent of what I do is staged. That's part of the business I'm in. And I really do make an effort not to do something stupid that will put me in the other five percent. My parents are still breathing, and I don't want to embarrass them or have to explain myself."

She hugged her shawl close to ward off the chill. He slid an arm around her and pulled her to his warmth. "I should have remembered what it was like," she said. "My year as Rose Queen was pretty intrusive. I should think for you it would be much, much worse. I thought the year would be fun with gowns, riding on a float and wearing a tiara."

"What turned you off?"

She wasn't really turned off as much as she was disappointed with people. "People asked me the strangest questions, like, 'What are you going to do if you have to go to the bathroom and you're on the float?' I'm thinking, 'I don't want to think about that, and it isn't any of your business.'" She remembered she'd always been polite, but vague. "And another one was, 'How does it feel to represent your people?'"

He nodded and looked understanding. "I get that one, too."

"I wasn't the first African American Rose Queen."

"And I wasn't the first black talk show host," he commiserated. "But still, someone will start asking around, looking for dirt on you."

"Fortunately I didn't have that problem." What dirt would the media have been able to find on her? She'd led a sheltered life. As Rose Queen, her schedule had included over a hundred public appearances and events; she'd had no time to get into trouble.

"I don't recall any scandals associated with Rose Queens."

"I don't know of any, either. Pasadena is many things, but the areas they are most proud of are the parade, the queen and her court, and this museum. I think if a person were to besmirch any one of those things, there would be pain."

He laughed. She liked the rich, deep sound of his real laugh.

The air was sweetly scented with flowers. Greer took a deep breath, feeling peace descend on her. Whenever she needed to be grounded, this was where she came. Often she brought her notebooks and sketched different flowers as she wandered through the garden. Just being here restored her. Sometimes she would visit the most famous resident sculpture, Rodin's *The Thinker*.

As they sat there on the bench, other walkers wandered through the garden. The sound of music drifted out from the museum behind them.

"Did you know that flowers speak their own language?" When he gave her a look, she explained. "For instance, the red rose means beauty and love." Which was probably why she loved red roses the best.

"What about yellow?" Daniel asked.

"Jealousy and envy. And daisies stand for innocence," she added.

"How do you know this?"

"A book called *The Language of Flowers*. It was published in the 1800s. My mother has a copy." Greer adored the book. She'd spent many a drama-filled teenage evenings reading the poetry and studying the meanings.

"Remind me to check with you before I send you flowers."

"Are you planning on sending me flowers?"

He grinned at her. "Maybe."

She smiled happily. Despite her years designing and decorating floats, she'd never gotten over her love of flowers. She inhaled their scent and turned to him. He surprised her by sliding his arms around her and pulling her close for a kiss.

His lips were warm and seductive against hers. For a second she was too surprised to respond. Quickly, though, hunger for this man filled her, and she pressed herself into the kiss, responding eagerly.

But as she opened her mouth to his, he pulled away. "I didn't mean to do that."

"Why not?" She certainly did not have a problem with it, and wondered why he did.

He shook his head. "I don't know...but I liked it."

"Me, too." She sat back with a slight frown. "So, how did I measure up?"

"To what?"

She traced his lips with her finger. "Your lips have kissed some of the most beautiful women in the world. How do I measure up to them?"

"I'm not sure how to answer your question." He tilted his head to look at her intently.

"You have this reputation to maintain. I don't fall into the category of your usual playmates."

"The only reason you asked me out was to compare yourself to the other women I've dated?"

How was she going to get herself out of this? The kiss was so unexpected and her response had been so intense, she felt the need to put up a barrier between herself and Daniel. "I was a little curious. You're a nice guy, so please don't be offended."

"I'm not offended. But I'm curious, too. Why do you feel I would compare you to all these other women?"

She didn't know how to answer him, so she avoided the question. She glanced at her watch. "Look at the time. I think I'd better get home." She started to stand, but he caught her arm, pulled her back and kissed her again.

She felt as though her insides were melting. Heat

flared through her, and she wound her arms around his neck. *Don't stop. Don't stop. Don't stop.* The kiss deepened. She groaned low in her throat.

When he pulled away, his eyes had darkened, and he wore a glimmer of a smile.

"Just so you know," he said, "there is no comparison. And you take that however you need to." He stood and pulled her to her feet. "Now let's get you home."

He pulled out his phone and called the limo driver. "We're ready to leave."

A minute later, Daniel handed her into the limo and started to close the door.

"Aren't you coming?" she asked.

He shook his head. "See her safely to her door," he told the driver before he turned back to her. "Don't worry about me. I'll get home on my own."

He walked away while Greer stared after him open-mouthed. This was not how she wanted the evening to end.

Daniel fumed while he waited for Nick to pick him up. He paced back and forth, occasionally sitting on a bench and watching the other people leave as the exhibition wound down. Twenty minutes later, his brother turned into the parking lot and stopped at the curb.

"What happened?" Nick asked after Daniel buckled his seat belt and glared at him. "That is not your happy face."

"I think I was just insulted."

"Did you run into Logan at the affair? The two of you trade insults all the time."

"I kissed Greer," Daniel said, "and she wanted to know how she compared to all the other women I've kissed."

"Ouch. What did you tell her?"

"I didn't say anything. I just kissed her again, put her in the limo and sent her home." He'd never had a woman question his ego before. Kissing Greer had rocked his world, and he thought it had rocked hers, as well. He'd enjoyed every moment of the kiss and the feel of her in his arms. He'd loved the faint fragrance of her perfume and the softness of her hair. "In fact, I want to kiss her again."

"You sound like you're falling in love."

"Not at all," he said emphatically. "I just like her, that's all. She's different." Maybe too different, he realized. What would he have in common with her?

"Different in what way?" Nick had braked for a light. Now the light changed, and he zoomed through the intersection.

"She's intelligent."

"You've dated a lot of smart women."

"She's talented."

"You've been there and done that, too."

Daniel glared at his brother. "You are not helping."

Nick burst out laughing. "Maybe she was just curious. I think you're overreacting."

"I'm not used to having my actions questioned in such a way."

"What you're used to are women who are grateful for your attention. Welcome to the real world, bro."

Daniel slumped back in the seat. "As if you've been swimming in the reality pool lately. Broadway star. TV star. Tennis star."

"I have a reputation to maintain." He turned onto the entrance to the 210 freeway, merged into traffic. Even at night, the freeways in Los Angeles were crowded.

"And I don't?"

"Reality in Hollywood is at a premium. Everything is already an illusion. Half the dates I have are for show. Greer might just have been questioning the illusion. She may feel uncomfortable in your world. How many times do we get asked to do things for business that make us uncomfortable, and we do them anyway? And why? 'Cause we like a big, comfortable house and our big, cushy cars. We like swiping our credit cards and knowing there's money in our accounts. We listened to Mom and Dad talk about how poor they were when they first started out, and we work damn hard not to be that poor."

"Fair enough. I feel like I've just been lectured." He'd missed his brother while Nick had been in New York. And now that he was home for good, he had someone to talk to. Like many twins, they were closer than most siblings.

"I'm channeling Mom. She and I had this conversation a couple of months ago." Nick exited the freeway. His career had been pretty much in New York, where Broadway actors didn't seem to spend their lives in the same fishbowl that Hollywood actors did. Broadway was considered more sophisticated, more of an art form.

"You're the one who wanted to come home."

"I wanted to be closer to family," Nick said. "And let's face it. I'm making three times the money and doing way less work. But people are now up in my business every time I step out of the house."

"Don't I know that. Is it worth it?"

Nick thought for a few moments. "Yeah. I think so. I enjoy what I do, and the challenge of choreographing new stuff weekly keeps me on my toes. So, what are you going to do about Greer?"

"I don't know. She confuses me. And I don't like to be confused." Daniel looked out the window at the night streets. Even at midnight, Los Angeles was restless and awake.

"Nobody does. You're never sure in our business if someone has an agenda."

"Are you saying celebrities can't fall in love?" Daniel studied his brother.

"We fall in and out of love all the time. But Greer is different, unique. Even though I haven't met her, I sense she's got dedication."

"A part of her isn't impressed with who I am." That was hard to admit for Daniel; he enjoyed the perks of being who he was.

"Does she impress you?"

Daniel thought about that for a few seconds. "A lot."

"It's time for you to grow up, bro. You've been

living every man's fantasy—beautiful women, cool friends, hot cars. What do you really want?"

Daniel wasn't certain he liked this grilling, and he probably wouldn't have been taking it from anybody but his twin. "I originally wanted to be in broadcast journalism, but I ended up more a talk show host. And I love it." His voice trailed away. He hadn't answered his brother's question. "I have the respect of my peers, and I get paid." But he had to admit, something was missing. He tried to pin down what, but his mind kept splintering away.

"But something's missing," Nick said for him.

"Are you crazy?"

Nick laughed as he turned into the driveway of Daniel's modest Glendale home and put his car in Park. "Success is fun only when you have someone to share and enjoy it with—or lord it over. You can't lord it over our sisters and brothers because we're all successful, too. So I think you're looking for someone to share it with."

"I don't think so," Daniel said, denial heavy in his voice. He stared at the front door of his home, wondering if Greer would like it. Her own home had been such a surprise with its colorful paint and traditional furniture.

"Look at Nina. Secretly we all knew Carl was her starter husband, but we didn't tell her, and look what happened."

"She's our sister. Why didn't we say something?"

"Because there would have been pain," Nick said with a chuckle. "But look at her now. She's as happy as our parents, and would any of us have picked a man like Scott for her? She found him on her own, and we all know he's the right choice. And now that one of us is really settled, we're starting to think."

"Are *you* thinking about a forever woman?"

"No, but maybe you are. With Greer."

Daniel had no answer for that. "I have to go." He scrambled out of the car, determined to get as far away from his twin as possible.

"I can't go on the show tomorrow."

Greer sat at her drafting table, a tray of water-color paints to one side and a half-done float design on the heavy paper taped to the tilted top. She'd been thinking about next year even though the theme for the next year's parade wouldn't be announced until January. Anything to take her mind off Daniel Torres. Her plan wasn't working.

"You should go on the show," she told Chelsea. "It's time for you to talk about the flowers anyway."

Chelsea grinned at her sister, eyes slightly narrowed. "What's going on, Greer?"

"I can't talk about it."

"Of course you can. I'm your sister."

"Don't play the sister card on me unless you're willing to help me and go on the show tomorrow."

"Tell me," Chelsea ordered. She looked composed and professional in her beige pantsuit that complimented her light cinnamon-colored skin. She'd wound a red-and-blue scarf about her neck and complimented it with red earrings and bracelets. As always, Chelsea was a knockout.

"I kind of… I kind of…kissed him last night." Greer covered her face with her hands, reliving the kiss once more. She'd spent all night dreaming about Daniel and the way his smooth mouth had felt on hers. In the dream she'd let him get a lot further than just a kiss, and the memory brought heat to her cheeks.

"He's a good-looking man. No one would blame you."

Greer put her head down on her drafting table and resisted the desire to bang her forehead against it. "He freaked me out. One moment we're talking and the next he's kissing me, and what do I do? I'm thinking about how I measure up to all those women. He's kissed some of the most beautiful women in the world and…and I'm just me."

"And you told him that, didn't you?" Chelsea reached over and patted Greer's head. "You know you can't be honest with men. Not until you get some mileage on them."

Greer pushed her hair back. "I didn't mean to ask him, but I kept feeling as though the kiss was a test run for something. Or maybe I was testing him."

"This is what happens when you date one guy for five years," Chelsea replied with a little *tsk* in her tone. "You get no baseline."

"Do I have to remind you that you're the one getting a divorce?" Greer had stayed with Roy because he'd been safe and comfortable and was willing to tolerate her desire to grow her family's business. He'd asked nothing of her, and until the day he told her he had found someone else, she'd asked nothing of him. Daniel Torres was a totally different type of man. His type A personality overshadowed her own type A personality—and that was speaking volumes.

Chelsea shrugged. "Christopher isn't to blame for why our marriage went south. I got married too young."

"And you're a workaholic."

"Just like you," Chelsea said cheerfully. She poured a mug of hot water and dangled a tea bag in it. When the tea was brewed to her satisfaction, she added a touch of sugar and cream to it and sat down on the sofa.

"So you won't take over for me tomorrow?" Greer asked her.

"Not a chance."

"You're a great sister," she groaned. "What about Rachel? She could go on the show and talk about how much a good float can cost."

Chelsea shook her head. "People don't want to know how much a float costs. They just want it to be beautiful. The audience wants to see you, the former Rose Queen who changes the fantasy into reality."

"It's going to be awkward," Greer said.

"Life is already awkward. And what fun would it be if it wasn't?"

"Fun for you."

Chelsea laughed. "Always. What kind of sister would I be if I didn't enjoy your discomfort? Besides, I have a meeting tomorrow with the rep from Trident Airlines."

"Your meeting is at two in the afternoon."

"I have to get ready. He's hot and I'm looking for my transition man."

Greer groaned. How was she going to face Daniel? She'd questioned his masculinity. Why couldn't she have just kept her mouth shut? As much as she had enjoyed the kiss, she'd felt uncomfortable and needed to protect herself.

She didn't want to, but she needed to apologize. In a way, she'd acted badly. She'd never done something like that before, but her own sense of honesty had got in the way.

"Got to go, sis," Chelsea said. She kissed Greer on the cheek and exited the office, leaving Greer to tackle the best way to apologize on her own.

Chapter 3

Daniel put his pen down, unable to concentrate. He'd arrived at the studio around four thirty for the 5:00 a.m. start to his show, as usual, and had downed several gallons of coffee. But it wasn't the caffeine that had him jittery this morning. While the weather, traffic and international news were on, he'd taken the opportunity to step off the set and slip back into his office before the next segment—the weekly update on the float. He tried to push away the apprehension he felt at seeing Greer again. His long discussion with Nick had not helped at all.

The door to his office crept open. He glanced up to find Greer standing in the doorway. In one hand she held a bouquet of roses in a dozen different colors, and in the other a box of Belgian chocolates. "These are for you." She thrust the roses and the candy at him. "And I'm sorry for my crazy."

Daniel stood, totally and completely charmed by her gesture. He accepted the gifts. "You don't have anything to apologize for. I was presumptuous."

"And I was uncomfortable." She looked relieved that he wasn't holding anything against her.

He opened a cabinet under the bar and found a vase for the flowers, which he set on the corner of his desk. Then he opened the box of candy and handed her one.

She shook her head. "I just brushed my teeth and I've already been warned not to eat or drink anything before our segment."

He closed the box and set it next to the flowers. "Thank you for these."

"I didn't want to come today. I was worried…"

"I knew you'd be here." He brushed aside her comment. "Let's go knock 'em dead."

He led her out onto the set, and she took a seat on the sofa. Her smile was stiff, and her posture told him she needed to relax.

"Don't look at the camera," he whispered. "Look at me."

She smiled gratefully.

The director knelt under the camera, one hand raised. "Five, four, three, two…" He closed his hand into a fist.

"Good morning, Los Angeles." Daniel's greeting was accompanied by applause from the live audience. He couldn't understand why anyone would be here by four in the morning in order to sit in the audience. But they had arrived, and now he had to give these people a show. "With us again this morning is Miss Greer Courtland from Courtland Float Designs to give us an update on our Rose Parade entry. Miss Courtland."

She'd given the director drawings that flashed on the screen as she talked about the flowers that would be the final decoration on his float.

"The floats can use only organic material."

"So no toilet paper like we used in the days when we were in high school," Daniel put in.

Greer laughed and visibly relaxed. "No toilet paper. The butterflies will contain a mixture of seeds for the bodies, red, yellow and green carnations for the inside area of the wings and dark red roses for the outer areas." She went on to explain how the flowers would add so much weight that the floats could easily double or triple in weight, and each pound needed to be accounted for.

"Do people cheat?"

She looked at him. "What do you mean?"

"What happens if the flowers don't come in the right colors?"

"There's a lot of last-minute improvising. Nothing ever goes smoothly."

"Like what?"

"Floats break down. The weather is uncomfortable. Sometimes flowers get held up in customs."

"Where are these coming from?"

"All over. My family has contracts with flower growers in Venezuela, Southeast Asia, Florida, Louisiana, even my parents' next-door neighbor, Mrs. Allenworth. She was a Rose Queen in the sixties, and she has an amazing garden and greenhouse. My parents use her flowers every year as a way to honor her commitment to the parade ideals."

"Rose Queens have ideals?"

"Yes, we do," Greer said. "We represent the whole concept of the parade and the city of Pasadena. And flowers have their own meanings as well."

"What does a bouquet of different colors mean?" He couldn't help asking the question. It had been on his mind ever since she'd walked in with the colorful bouquet.

She glanced sharply at him. "Color coordination is a good thing."

Not the answer he expected. So…what could he ask?

"Give us the meanings of some of the flowers."

"Red roses symbolize love. Peonies symbolize compassion. If your viewers are interested, they can go to the Courtland website. We have links to direct them to that information."

"Thank you."

She talked a little more about the float and the staging area at the Rose Bowl parking lot, letting viewers know that volunteers were always appreciated. He suspected she'd garner her fair share of volunteers from the audience, who seemed to love her.

All too soon her segment ended. When she left the stage, for a moment Daniel wanted to call her back. But he had a show to finish.

When it finally ended, he wished everyone a happy Thanksgiving and told them he would see them again Thanksgiving morning with tips on cooking the perfect turkey.

He walked back to his office and opened the door to find his sister Nina sitting on the sofa, the box of chocolate open and one piece halfway to her mouth. She looked chic and fashionable in a dark gray suit and a peacock-blue blouse.

"Nina!"

"Good chocolate," she said popping the piece in her mouth and licking her fingers. "These are terrific and made right here in Pasadena. To think I've been ordering my chocolate direct from Belgium."

"I thought you planned to stay in Reno with Scott's family for Thanksgiving."

"I did, until I got this funky phone call from Nick."

"Why did Nick call you?"

"Apparently, someone we both know is having a love crisis."

"Nick's in love?" Daniel kept his tone teasing.

"He thinks you are."

"I'm not in love." Daniel sat down next to his sister and popped a piece of chocolate into his mouth. If he kept it full, he might not have to answer her questions.

Nina took the box away from him and closed it firmly. "It's that cute parade girl, isn't it? I've seen the way you look at her when you're together on camera. You can barely form a sentence. You're pretty funny, and the whole nation is watching your courtship on TV. Oh, big brother, your game is shameful."

Daniel glared at her. "Maybe you need to head back to Reno."

"And miss the opportunity to talk madness about you? Never." Nina burst out laughing. "I don't often get the chance to tweak any of my brothers." She leaned over and kissed his cheek. "Especially my older brothers. And I hear the flowers—" she held her hand out to the vase of roses "—are from her, too."

"Claudia told you."

"She did," Nina said with a chuckle.

"I need to have a talk with my personal assistant about boundaries."

"We're siblings. There are no personal boundaries between us. Everything is up for family fodder."

Daniel groaned. *Why me?* He was much happier when everyone's attention was on someone else.

"Do you know what a bouquet of different colored roses means?" she teased.

"I'm sure you're going to tell me."

"It means mixed feelings in the way that says, 'I don't know how I feel yet, but I like you enough to bring you roses.'"

"How do you know that?" he asked.

"I love reading Regency romances when I have the time, and the meaning of flowers is important in those stories."

"You've always been the busybody in our family."

"I get it from Mom," she said.

"Go start your own family, then."

"Already done, big bro." She touched her tummy.

"What?"

"Scott and I came to make a formal announcement to the family. That's why we changed our plans and headed here for Thanksgiving."

"Is it okay for you to fly?"

"I've been pregnant for five minutes. The nugget and I are fine." She patted his cheek.

"Should you be eating chocolate?"

"I didn't prematurely announce my pregnancy to distract you from your love life."

"A man can hope."

She laughed again. "Oh, bro, we're going to have so much fun. I want you to take me out to wherever she is and introduce me."

"Now?"

"Yes. I have things to do." She stood, grabbed her purse and tapped one foot as she waited for him. "Come on, bro. Clock's ticking."

"I thought I was the one who was supposed to check out your potential dates."

Nina laughed. "You were nowhere around while I was making my move on Scott."

"Probably a good thing. Your ex-commando husband can probably twist me like a soggy pretzel."

Nina grabbed him by the arm and tugged him to the door. "Ha-ha. You're funny. Now let's go."

Greer perched on a stool, her drawing pad in hand, beside Daniel's float. It was still a skeleton of aluminum screen and plastic foam atop the motorized chassis, but not for long.

"Okay," Chelsea said. "1-A is red rose petals."

Greer marked 1-A on her drawing and added the information to the legend in the corner.

"Chia seeds for 1-B," Chelsea called out.

The floats had been moved to the Rose Bowl parking lot and tucked into a corner. Here the final decorations would be added and, on the morning of the parade, the float staged.

"Bark for 1-C," Chelsea yelled.

The tiniest dimensions were recorded on Greer's drawing. When completed, the drawing would be copied and handed out to the volunteers so they would know what went where. Nothing was left to chance.

Chelsea crawled around on the float, calling out directions, until a commotion sounded behind them. She paused, looking up. "Well, look who's here," she said, hopping down from the chassis.

Greer followed her sister's gaze…and felt her throat grow dry when she saw who approached them.

"It's Daniel Torres," Chelsea said, "and it looks like he brought reinforcements."

Greer sighed. "This isn't going to go well, is it?"

The woman with Daniel was tall and slim and so beautiful Greer's breath caught in her throat. She wore designer jeans and a loose-fitting peasant blouse that looked perfect on her.

Daniel made his way toward Greer, the woman in tow. "Hi," he said with a wave as he approached. "This is my sister Nina. Nina, this Greer, and the woman over there is Greer's sister Chelsea. Nina is going to work some PR magic."

"I am," Nina said. She looked pleased.

Greer hopped down from her stool and held out a hand to Nina. "Pleased to meet you."

Nina looked her up and down, a delighted look on her face. "I've been enjoying your segments with my brother. If you ever consider a career change, I can get you a great hosting gig. *About Town with Greer.* How does that sound?"

Greer was too bemused to answer right away. "I'm fine right where I am. I'm doing what I love."

"Of course you are." She waved a hand at the float. "It's creative, beautiful and looks like fun, and I know exactly what you mean. You have passion." She took the drawing pad away from Greer and studied the drawing. "And talent." Daniel's phone rang and Nina glanced back at him. "Go ahead and answer that. We'll keep ourselves busy."

"That's what I'm afraid of," Daniel muttered.

She pushed him away as his phone chimed again. Daniel put his phone to his ear and walked away. She turned back to Greer. "You have him on the ropes. Congratulations."

Greer didn't know what to say; she was speechless. She thought her sister was going to save her when Chelsea walked over. Then she saw the grin on her sister's face as she leaned in to Nina.

"Isn't that the truth," Chelsea said. "Let's dissect."

Greer glared at Chelsea. "You're my sister. You're supposed to be on my side."

Chelsea shook her head. "I'm on the side that will provide me with the most amusement."

Greer wanted to stomp away. She didn't want to

hear her life being dissected, but Nina caught her by the arm. "Don't you want to hear Daniel's secrets? I know them all."

Pausing, Greer studied Daniel's sister. A gleam in the woman's eyes told Greer she was not going to get away. "I don't want to hear his secrets."

"You're sucking all the fun out of this for me. My brother hasn't been confused by a woman since he was seven years old and in love with the girl next door. If I remember correctly, her name was Debra Sands, maybe Sandleman. Something like that." She shook her head. "Debbie had the prettiest red hair and green eyes and she was fifteen years old and his first older woman."

Greer glanced at Daniel. He'd retreated to the open entrance, the phone to his ear, a frown on his face as he listened to the caller.

"I'm feeling a little uncomfortable."

"Don't," Nina said with a huge grin. "We Torreses love to taunt each other. There are seven of us kids, so that's a lot of fodder to be consumed."

"How do you keep track of everybody?" Greer asked curiously.

"Name tags," Nina replied. "And a good spread-sheet. I had enough blackmail material on my broth-ers by the time I was ten to keep them all in line until the year 2112."

Greer burst out laughing. "Didn't they do the same to you?"

"They tried." She winked at Greer. "Daniel and I were the best ones at talking ourselves out of trouble.

And when he couldn't, he blamed Nick for every-thing. Poor Nick got blamed for dyeing our mom's dog pink and purple. But that was me. He got blamed for the reproductive system mural that ended up in the den. That was Daniel. Fortunately for us, Nick was good-natured about it. He got me back when he glued my braids together. My mother had to cut them off. And I was so traumatized I never grew my hair out again."

"Harsh," Chelsea said. "The worst thing my sisters ever did to me was hide my senior prom dress an hour before my date was to arrive."

"And you got me back by welding my favorite necklace to the hood of mom's Cadillac. Mom wasn't amused, though. It's a good thing the Rose Queens aren't allowed to keep their crowns or you would have used that instead."

"Children can be so cruel to each other," Nina said, but it was clear from her laugh that she wouldn't have had it any other way. She turned her attention to the enormous float. "So, explain to me what you both are doing."

"We're laying out what flowers go where, and where the bodies will go." Chelsea said, pointing at the chairs on the chassis. One held a photo of Daniel, and two others contained photos of Nick's face and his dance partner. The fourth had a sheet of paper with a question mark. Daniel still hadn't told them who would be the fourth person on the float.

"We have to distribute weight as evenly as we can," Greer explained. She walked around the float.

Then she scrambled onto the chassis and started to explain the hydraulics of the butterflies.

Greer leaned against the float, watching Daniel, still talking on his phone while Chelsea talked to Nina. He spoke rapidly, his frown increasing. She wanted to rub the frown away and wondered what was going on that so consumed his attention for the moment.

He was such a sexy man, she couldn't take her eyes off him. So what was holding her back from going after him? He was attractive and kind, not at all what she'd expected, and he came from a good family. Her mother had once told her that nice people came from nice families. Greer had met Manny and Grace Torres, and they were incredibly nice. So was Nina. What she'd heard about the rest of the family told her they were all good people, too.

What made her so uncomfortable in getting involved with Daniel was the public scrutiny. She had endured the same scrutiny during her months as Rose Queen, which had been very stressful. In addition to all the public appearances, she'd been subjected to more attention being an African American Rose Queen, not to mention she still had to maintain her GPA in school. Though she'd enjoyed her time in the spotlight, she'd been delighted when it had finally ended. Being in the public eye made her more uncomfortable than she'd thought she'd be. Her neighbor, Mrs. Allenworth, had trained her, imparting the wisdom of her own time as Rose Queen, which had been difficult as well. Mrs. Allenworth had been Rose

Queen in 1968, a time when women were questioning their traditional roles and some saw the position of Rose Queen as being counterproductive to the advancement of women. With all of her grace, poise and intelligence, she had staved off the criticism, declaring that as a feminist, being the Rose Queen gave her unique power and versatility.

For Greer's part, while she loved what the Rose Queens stood for, her fifteen minutes of fame had been fourteen-and-a-half minutes too long.

Even though she was not a big follower of celebrity news, like anyone who lived in Los Angeles, Greer couldn't help but be inundated by it. The one thing that always bothered her was how the women were judged on such trivial things as their appearance, their weight, their dating life. No one seemed to care what kind of people these women were, what was in their hearts or in their minds, unless it was something catty or outrageous.

She was still staring at Daniel when he ended his phone call. She averted her eyes when he headed back toward her.

"That was my producer," he told her. "He wants to do a segment here. Anything interesting coming up?"

She thought for a second. "We need to schedule a safety drill. Not everyone does, but my parents believe in being prepared for the worst."

"A safety drill! Why?"

"Because one must learn proper exiting strategies in case there's a float emergency."

"What kind of float emergencies can there be?"

"Fire. Earthquake. Stampede."

He frowned at her. "What kind of stampede?"

"Horses. People."

"You're making this up."

"Maybe," she said, stifling a grin.

Chelsea had wandered over, having finished her tour. "The great horse stampede of 1979 never made it to TV," she said, shaking her head.

"The horror," Greer cried. "The horror."

"Neither one of you was born in 1979," Daniel scoffed, "so how would you know?"

She leaned toward him, her tone confiding. "It's a thing that only insiders know and has been kept secret for decades. No one wants to frighten the spectators."

"Now I know you're pulling my leg," Daniel said, taking a step back, doubt on his face.

"Ask around," Chelsea said. "There are whispers."

He stared at them. Behind Chelsea, Nina had clapped a hand over her mouth, her eyes twinkling.

Greer, too, could hardly contain herself.

"Enough," Daniel said. "So, when are you scheduling this 'safety drill'?" He held up his hands in finger quotes.

"Sometime next week. I can only get your brother on Tuesday or Thursday morning. Since he's going to be on the float with his dance partner, they need to be a part of this, too."

"The film crew can be here on either day. Just let me know."

Greer nodded. She felt a little guilty teasing Daniel, but only a little. Safety was always a big concern, especially after the year Rachel had broken her ankle fleeing a float when the engine had caught fire. After that, they'd had safety drills, and her parents had made the drills as fun as possible because they didn't want anyone worrying about what could go wrong during the parade rather than enjoying it. And something always went wrong.

"Do I need anything in particular like a hazmat suit, fire extinguishers, or an emergency medical team standing by?" Daniel seemed to realize he was being teased.

Greer grinned. "You're getting into the spirit of things."

"I can cooperate."

"Okay, then. I think we're done." She turned toward the float. "You have a good day. I enjoyed meeting your sister."

Daniel grabbed her arm. "You and I are far from done." She stopped and turned to glare at him. When she started to speak, he put his finger on her lips. "What are you doing tomorrow for Thanksgiving?"

"I have family obligations. My parents take Thanksgiving very seriously. We have to eat until we fit into the next size pants, and that takes pacing."

"That sounds like you do Thanksgiving right."

"We do, but you're going to be restricted on your own diet. Don't you dare gain an ounce. I can't have you unbalancing the float."

He frowned at her. "Are you teasing me again?"

"No. Weight distribution is a very serious issue. It's for real."

"She's been known to hack off some thigh fat," Chelsea put in.

"Your face says 'I'm kidding,' but her face," Daniel pointed at Greer, "says not so much."

Chelsea just shrugged. "Making sure her weight requirement is met is Greer's favorite thing during float season."

"Have you ever gone over?"

"Never," Greer said, daring him to be the first.

"Well, thank you for the weird conversation. I've got to get going now. Nina."

Nina smiled at him. "I think I'm going to stay awhile. I'm getting ideas on how to spin this, and I need to work on them. You go on. I'll catch you at the restaurant tomorrow."

He left without a backward glance. Greer watched him leave the tent, half of her wanting to go after him and apologize. Something must have showed on her face.

"You have truly amused me," Nina said.

"I have? Thank you."

"I can make you a star."

"In our world, she's already a star," Chelsea put in. "She's the Angelina Jolie of float designers."

"Our world is very small," Greer said as she leaned against the float.

"Never underestimate the power of being the biggest fish in a little pond. That's who runs the show." Nina perched herself on the side of the float. She patted the spot next to her. "Now come here and tell me everything."

"You don't take no for an answer, do you?"

"Never. I'm on speed dial for ninety percent of Hollywood. I get the job done."

"You're beautiful enough to be in front of the camera. Why aren't you?"

"I fix problems. I don't make them," Nina said. "Now come here and sit next to me and tell me how you are keeping my brother on the ropes. I've never seen him so confused before." She didn't even try to hide the grin that split her face.

Thanksgiving Day for most people was food, football and family. For the Torres family, Thanksgiving was different. Daniel's father closed the restaurant to normal business and opened it up for the homeless who came in droves to be served the best turkey dinner ever. The whole family pitched in except his mother and his sister Lola, who stayed home to cook their own Thanksgiving dinner, which would be served to the family later.

Daniel waited tables, smiling when he recognized some regular customers who volunteered their time to help out, as well. Logan participated, too, bussing tables. As the last diners left the restaurant, Manny Torres closed and locked the doors.

Most of the tables had already been cleared. Logan brought in a container of dirty dishes. Daniel stacked dishes in the dishwasher while Nick hand-washed what didn't fit. They'd been doing the same routine for years, so it went smoothly.

"I heard your date to the Norton Simon was a

bust," Logan said, a grin on his face as he sidled up to Daniel .

"From Nina or Nick?" Daniel asked.

"Nina keeps secrets. Nick's the blabbermouth." Logan helped Daniel stack the last of the dishes in the dishwasher. "Step aside. Give me the field. You know how much I like the chase."

Daniel looked at his friend. "Why do we compete over everything?" Usually it was all in good fun, but Logan chasing after Greer annoyed Daniel in a way he hadn't predicted.

"If you have four rocks, I have to have five," Logan said. "It's the nature of our friendship and makes for good ratings for our shows."

That was so true. And yet their rivalry had the strongest of friendships behind it. "To be honest, it wasn't really a bust. I think Greer is uncomfortable dating a celebrity."

"Yeah," Logan said. "She looks at us like we're real guys and not a meal ticket. And that's a novelty for us. 'Cause deep down inside, in those dark places we don't like to acknowledge, the reason we went into this business is that we get what we want when we want it."

Daniel shrugged. "I'm not ashamed to admit it. We worked hard to get this life, and there's nothing wrong with enjoying the perks. But Greer doesn't want to be a perk." And that was what confused Daniel. He'd been dating starlets and beautiful women for so long that he expected all women to be more interested in his status or his money. And because

Greer wasn't, that altered the game. He was going to have to change if he wanted her. He did want her. He wanted her so bad his heart ached. "I'm not throwing in the towel yet."

Logan grinned. "Sweet. Neither am I. You have to admit, she's one hell of a woman."

Daniel sighed. He didn't know how to proceed. He wanted to consult with his mother, but what grown man would admit that? Grace Torres was as cool as any mother could be, and her place was a judgment-free zone. As long as he didn't talk sex with her, she gave pretty good advice. He was going to have to bite the bullet. Greer was worth it.

"You're going to talk to your mom, aren't you?" Logan asked. He snapped the dishwasher closed and turned it on. "You have that look on your face."

"I have no secrets from you, do I?"

Logan shook his head. "Very few. I will say one thing. If not for your mother, I would be living in a bottle of tequila." Logan's career-ending injury had been the worst for a quarterback. Besides a severe concussion, he'd broken every bone in his throwing hand. "Your mom is better than four therapists put together. She got me back on my feet, back into life, and pointed me in the right direction. All my parents did was complain that life was so unfair. But not your mom. Her advice saved my life."

Daniel knew his mother was someone special. "Yeah, I'm going to talk to her," he admitted. "As soon as possible."

Logan grinned. "So am I."

Daniel glared at him. That was just wrong. "She's my mother. She bore me."

Logan's grin widened. "You're right, but she chose me."

Daniel shook his head. Yeah, he and Logan could compete at just about anything.

Chapter 4

"I didn't expect to find you here on a Saturday, and so late in the afternoon," Daniel said, lounging in the doorway to Greer's office.

She swiveled on her stool, blinking. She'd been so engrossed in what she was doing, she never heard him opening the door. Her heart started racing and her nerve endings tingled. What this man did to her. Not that she was going to let him know that. "Then why did you come here?"

She put down her colored pencil. It was time to stop working on the float design coming to life on the paper spread across her drafting table. She hadn't intended to come in on a Saturday, but an idea had been nagging at her, and she'd wanted to get it down on paper before she lost it.

"Your sister Rachel asked me to come in for a budget meeting. The price of orchids apparently went up thirty percent because of some storm in Venezuela that destroyed the stock and the greenhouse they were growing in, and Rachel wanted approval for an emergency order out of Louisiana." Daniel entered and glanced around.

"Yeah, like I told you, last-minute emergencies always crop up. Mother Nature is at her finest this year." Greer started to put her colored pencils away. She closed the tin lid and slid the box into a storage drawer. "She told you I was here?"

He nodded. "We've gotten off on the wrong foot, and I want to make it up to you."

That was an understatement. She slid off the stool, intrigued. She was going to let him, but she wanted him to work for it. "I'm listening."

"How about I show you the stars?"

"You mean a Hollywood party?" That was the last thing she wanted.

"No. Better than that. I'm going to show you the galaxy." He waved his hand over his head.

"That sounds mysterious." She was interested.

"Trust me." He held out his hand.

She hesitated, a dozen thoughts flitting through her head.

"Trust me," he coaxed again. "Do you have a warm coat?"

She opened the closet door and pulled out a thick jacket with a knit hat and gloves stuffed in a pocket. "I'm ready." A shiver of excitement spiraled through her. She had no idea what he had on his mind, but she was ready to go along with it.

"I collect cars," he said after they'd gotten in his car and were winding through the Pasadena streets toward the freeway to Glendale.

"You mean like Jay Leno or like Matchbox cars?"

"Funny. I mean like Jay Leno, though not so extensive."

"I'm not judging," she said lightly as she settled back against the leather upholstery of his Mercedes. She'd been surprised by his car. She would have thought he was Porsche kind of man, all fast and low to the ground. "Where are we going?"

"I need my truck."

She pictured him in a big Ford thundering down the highway with a Stetson perched on his head. She was so caught in her daydream, she barely watched the scenery. Like most times of the day or night, the freeway was jammed with traffic. Occasionally she caught a glimpse of houses with their Christmas lights on, reminding her she still had her Christmas shopping to do.

He pulled off the freeway, into an industrial area. After threading his way around the dark buildings, he parked in front of a warehouse. The huge door slowly rose. Lights came on inside, and she saw the bright shine of a dozen automobiles.

"Wow," she said, walking around a shimmering black Lamborghini. If not for a boyfriend in college who had been big into cars, she wouldn't have recognized any of them. She spotted a Tesla and the Porsche Spyder she'd originally imagined he'd drive.

An old racing Jaguar dominated a corner, as bright and shiny as the newer cars. A Dodge Ram truck hugged another corner.

"Boys and their toys," she said with a half smile.

"So you recognize them?" he teased.

"A few. I had a boyfriend once who loved his cars more than he loved me." And because his parents were a powerful Hollywood couple, he could indulge in his love of cars. Unfortunately, he also had a love of speed, which had not ended well. "What is that one over there? The silver one."

"It's a Koenigsegg."

"God bless you."

He laughed. "It's not a sneeze. It's a Swedish manufacturer. I almost didn't buy it, but it's so pretty. It had been in a bad accident, and I got it for a song. My body shop put it all back together." He ran a hand lightly along the fender.

"Sometimes I buy shoes that are just pretty, so I understand."

He walked over to a small office in the back and returned carrying a key. "Ready for your adventure?"

"I'm game," she said. To be honest, she would have followed him to the tundra to fight some wolves. And she hated the cold.

He pointed the remote at the truck and motioned her into it. She climbed in. Any larger and she would have needed a ladder. He drove the truck out and then excused himself to drive the Mercedes into the garage. Greer glanced around and noticed something in the truck bed. Something large and cylindrical under a huge canvas tarp held down with bungee cords crisscrossing the top. She wondered what was under it.

Darkness had fallen while they'd been in the garage, and it felt as if the temperature had dropped twenty degrees. Greer shivered a little while waiting for the heat to warm the cab.

When Daniel returned, she started to ask what was under the tarp, but didn't as he buckled his seat belt and put the truck in gear. She had something more important to ask him.

"Why did you ask me out?"

He grinned as he pulled out into traffic and headed toward the freeway. "Because you like me and it scares you."

She pondered his statement for a moment. "That's an unusual answer. Not what I was expecting." But he was right. And she hated it. She did like him, more than she wanted to. "You are pretty easy to like." And look at. "But you come with baggage. You have a high-pressure job. Your life is a fishbowl, and I don't want to be swimming in your fishbowl. I had enough exposure as Rose Queen. I loved it and hated it at the same time. When it was over, I was happy going back to my boring life."

He pulled off the freeway and turned onto the road leading into Griffith Park. At least now she knew where they were going. Before entering the park, he stopped at a small deli.

"Wait here," he said.

He left the motor running for the heat, but when he opened the door, cold air washed into the cab. She pulled her jacket more tightly about her. Daniel returned a few seconds later, a picnic basket in one hand.

"Are we having a feast?"

"Food stimulates the intellectual centers of the brain." He put the truck into gear and turned back onto the road leading to Griffith Park.

"So, we're having a picnic."

"We're having more than that," he said.

They continued in silence for a few miles. The road twisted, turned and climbed steadily up the side of a mountain. Occasionally Greer caught glimpses of the bright lights of Los Angeles glimmering below like stars. Was this what he meant when he told her he was going to show her the stars? She glanced up at the clear night sky.

He pulled into a picnic area and parked.

"Ready?" he asked.

"Yeah, I'm ready."

The cylindrical object in the bed of the truck turned out to be a telescope. Greer held the picnic basket while she watched him release the cords holding it in place and then shift the telescope to his shoulder. He led the way toward a large clearing with picnic tables and barbeque pits.

"What are you, an amateur astronomer on top of everything else?"

He hefted the telescope over his shoulder and

started walking toward an open grassy area. "Looking at the stars is practical as well as psychological."

"You must explain that to me."

He looked around the grassy area and lowered the telescope to the ground, placing the tripod legs carefully on the grass and making sure they were secure. "In my profession, it's never bad to understand that there are things bigger and more important than I will ever be."

Wow, that said a lot about him. She wasn't sure how she should take it, but she did like his humility.

He fussed with the telescope for several minutes, testing to make sure the legs were stable. He looked into the eyepiece at one end as he adjusted the lens.

Greer was impressed that he recognized his place in the world and he was comfortable with himself. She sat down on a picnic bench and stared at him. Suddenly he wasn't the arrogant, vain man she'd thought. He was better in real life than in her petty thoughts.

Her heart gave a little lurch and she felt an urge to take a long, deep look at this man. She had the feeling he'd never shown this side of himself to any of those exotically beautiful women he'd dated. She simply couldn't imagine a starlet in a sexy designer dress traipsing her way through the grass in six-inch heels.

He held out his hand. "This baby is a top-of-the-line Celestron telescope. Come here and give it try. I promised you stars." He made several more adjustments and then showed her how to use the telescope.

When she looked into the eyepiece, Greer caught

her breath. To one side, the full moon showed large and clear, with the depth of shadow easily seen. "So the moon isn't made of green cheese." She wondered how that odd idea had even gotten a start.

"Not at all," Daniel said. He leaned close to her, his breath warm on her cheek. "Now I'm going to move the scope slightly."

The telescope veered away from the moon, and what she saw next was a mystery. "What am I looking at?" Whatever she watched, it moved quickly. A meteor, perhaps?

"That's the International Space Station. It'll be gone shortly." He shifted the telescope again. "We were lucky to catch it. I worried I'd be too late tonight."

She saw stars. Hundreds of millions of stars. The night sky looked like black velvet stretched from one end of the horizon to the other. Greer's breath caught in her throat. "This is beautiful." She was overwhelmed by the splendor of the night sky she'd never stopped to look at before, as well as by a new sense of understanding about Daniel.

Greer remembered an introductory astronomy class she'd taken as an elective back in college. She'd thought it would be easy, just studying the constellations and recognizing them, but the class had been more about the history of astronomy and its evolution. Though she'd enjoyed it, she'd been a little disappointed. Giving her this incredible show, Daniel hadn't disappointed.

"I was hoping you'd like it."

"You don't show many women this, do you?" Again the image of a starlet in designer duds crossed her mind.

"The only women I've ever brought here are my mother and sisters."

"Hmm."

"Is that all you have to say?"

"I'm thinking about the significance of that statement."

He chuckled. He adjusted the telescope again. "Look again."

She looked into the eyepiece. "What am I looking at?"

"The North Star," he said. "In the Little Dipper."

For the next hour, he showed her different constellations. The universe was so large that Greer felt humbled beneath it. Later they sat at the picnic table, drinking wine and eating sandwiches.

"I find the night sky endlessly fascinating," Daniel said as he bit into his sandwich. "There is so much out there that is still a mystery."

"Like what?" Greer asked.

"In the last few years, several different types of stars have been discovered. Like the zombie stars. And the whirling dervish stars."

"*Zombie* isn't a term I'd associate with a star. And what is a whirling dervish?"

He grinned. "A star with a rotation is so fast that they are more egg-shaped than round. And zombie stars are white dwarf stars that had a weak supernova.

Parts of them are still active and look like they're coming back to life."

"You're kidding me."

He held up a hand. "Scout's honor. A zombie star was discovered by the Hubble telescope, or rather the image of one was discovered in 2014. Scientists will be studying it for years."

They sat in silence for a few minutes, finishing their sandwiches. Daniel looked so peaceful sitting there. The animation he showed while in front of the camera had been replaced by a relaxed pose and intense interest as he gazed at the dark sky.

"I'm surprised by this part of you," she told him. "Who knew you were interested in astronomy?" In fact, his interest in astronomy wasn't even mentioned in the Internet Movie Database. Greer had given in to temptation and looked him up.

"I know my job is to make lighthearted conversation and be entertaining. This is a part of me I get to keep just for me. And that's the way I want it. I share this with people I want to, not my TV viewers who don't need to know. And—" he paused for a second "—I need to be reminded that I'm not as important as I sometimes feel."

"You weren't kidding." To Greer this new knowledge she'd discovered about him made him more intriguing, adding new depths to his personality.

"My love of astronomy isn't glamorous or sexy." He took a sip of wine.

"You're wrong," Greer said in a husky voice. "It is to me."

He put down his wine down and leaned over to her. His kiss was light and tender, his lips soft against hers. His warm breath fanned over her cold cheek. Somehow this kiss was different from the first one amid the flowers and statues at the Norton Simon Museum. This kiss seemed more real, more right.

Greer should have known from the second she met him that they would eventually end up in her bed. He just snuck in under her radar and made her like him.

"Let's go home," he said.

"Yeah."

He jumped up and went to his telescope to disassemble it while Greer packed up the basket.

She was silent all the way back to her home, wondering if she should invite him in. She wanted to learn more about this man whose public image was so different from his private one. By the time he pulled into her driveway, she found the courage to ask him in for a nightcap.

"Are you sure?" he asked, studying her.

"I'm sure," she said and led him into her house. "You don't think I'm being too forward?" She took a moment to pet her cat and dogs, smiling as he joined her. Then he lifted her back to her feet and pulled her toward him.

Daniel kissed her, his lips warm and moist. "I don't think you're being too forward."

Daniel gently kissed her again, and she felt a deep need pulse through her. The kiss was more passionate, more intense, than any kiss she'd ever had.

He was truly a game changer. His gentleness surprised her in a pleasurable way. He seemed to want to take things slow. He trailed kisses down her neck, lifted her sweater up and off and gently stroked the swell of her breasts beneath her lacy red bra. Her nipples puckered.

She led him up the stairs to her bedroom. Once inside, he held her tight against him. Passion curled through her, leaving her breath ragged and thready. Slowly he leaned over and kissed the tops of each of her breasts. Then he reached behind her and un-hooked her bra.

Greer felt beautiful with him. Carefully he lowered the straps of her bra until her breasts were bare. She didn't even feel embarrassed being seminaked in front of him. His gaze slid down her body as he reached for the zipper on her jeans. When she was completely naked, he stepped back to look at her.

"You're beautiful," he said in breathless wonder.

She reached for his T-shirt and pushed it up to caress the smooth skin of his chest.

"I think you are, too," she said, sliding her fingers over his rigid nipples. He gasped, pulled his T-shirt off and reached down to unbutton his jeans.

She slipped off her sneakers and stepped out of her jeans. When she stood, Daniel was completely naked, and watching her. He ran his hands over her body, caressing her breasts, her hips, her butt. Greer's skin tingled every place he touched.

"I don't want to stop touching you." His voice came out as a half groan.

Greer rubbed her cheek against his smooth chin. "You don't need to."

"I have to get a condom."

Greer stroked his shoulders. "Hurry." Greer watched him take a condom out of his pocket. Had he anticipated how the night would end? She laughed, not caring. This was right. This was where they belonged.

"Where were we?" he asked.

She kissed him and pulled him down on the bed with her.

Daniel maneuvered their bodies until he lay on top of her, cradled in her thighs. Greer could feel his hardness against her. Moisture was already trickling down her, wetting her thighs.

He began to kiss his way down her body, starting with her cheek, then moving to her earlobe. He ran the tip of his tongue over the shell of her ear and nibbled his way to her neck. He took his time exploring her neck and shoulder. His silky skin moved over her, sending shudders through her. All she wanted was for him to take her to that place where pleasure was the only thing she experienced.

When his mouth found her breast and he took in a hard nipple, Greer cried out. He worked his tongue around her breast, laving every inch of it until she'd been thoroughly caressed. When he was finished with her breasts, he moved down her body until he found her navel. Ever so gently he swirled his tongue inside her belly button. She didn't think something like this could be such a turn-on, but the simple action sent waves of heat crashing through her. She moaned.

She was so ready, and he seemed content to just tease her. He licked the outside of her thigh, easing down toward her knee. When he lifted her leg high and blew his warm breath on the crook of her knee, she closed her eyes and gave herself over to the sensation. As wonderful as it all felt, she wanted him inside her, satisfying the need at her core. She leaned back on the bed and sighed. She had no doubt he wouldn't disappoint her.

He continued with his extremely slow, tortuous lovemaking. By the time he licked her instep, she bit down on her lip to stop from crying out.

Daniel rolled her on her stomach and started his reverse exploration. Greer was delirious with need by the time he found his way back to her shoulders. Quickly she rolled on her back and sat up. She took his face between her hands and kissed him hard. "Is it my turn yet?"

"Nope."

She cupped his cheek and pulled his mouth to hers. He pushed her thighs apart and slipped inside her, slowly, achingly slowly. For a second he stopped, as if he was waiting for her to accept him inside her. She didn't hesitate. Then, carefully, he buried himself fully inside her, and Greer knew she would never forget this moment.

He sighed. "You feel so good."

He moved inside her, her softness giving way to his hardness.

Daniel never took his eyes from hers. His hands moved over her slowly, and Greer relished every touch, every caress. He made love to her with such reverence, she felt she was the most precious thing in the entire world.

His jaw hardened as if he was holding back. She didn't want him to hold anything back from her, not now, not ever. "Love me harder," she urged him.

"I want it to last."

"It will." She wasn't sure if she was just talking about the lovemaking. "Don't hold back."

He thrust into her hard, and she could feel her orgasm begin to build. She raised her legs and wrapped them around him tighter. The tightness in her stomach built and burned through her. He lowered himself and pushed into her harder and harder until she flew over the edge, and a second or two later he came with her. The stars she'd seen in the night sky had nothing on the ones she'd seen in his arms.

Chapter 5

Daniel woke the next morning to bright sunshine streaming through the window. For a moment he didn't remember where he was as he looked at the cheerful bedroom with bright yellow paint and watercolors of Rose Parade floats on the walls. He was also conscious of a weight over his legs. A glance down showed a cat staring at him from her perch on his calves.

"Good morning, Scooter," Daniel said. He reached down to pet her, but the cat arched her back, hissed and jumped off the bed. As though that was their signal, the two dogs jumped up, their tails wagging.

"Pip and Roscoe, down," came Greer's command as she walked into the room. The two dogs glanced at her, then jumped down. "Coffee's almost ready. If you want a shower—" she pointed to a closed door at the other side of the room "—that's the bathroom."

She looked sexy in a black silk kimono, cinched tight around her waist with a long belt. He grabbed her and pulled her down on the bed, across his chest. "I do want a shower, but what I really want right now is you."

She grinned at him as his hand stole beneath the silk to caress her breast. She rolled to the side, the kimono gaping to show her smooth skin. She slid a leg up his. He took her nipple in his mouth, curling his tongue around it. Heat grew in him and she moaned. He untied the belt and pushed the kimono away from her body.

She was so beautiful.

"I want to make love to you all morning," he whispered against her lips. "Then we'll have lunch at Venice Beach. We can walk the boardwalk and watch the ocean." His mouth trailed down her neck, down past her belly… He knew where it was headed, and judging from her shaky breaths, so did she. He was flirting with the area above her thighs when her phone rang. "Don't answer that."

"I have to. Chelsea wouldn't call this early on a Saturday unless there's an emergency." She rolled to the side of the bed and reached for her phone. "What's up, Chelsea?" Greer listened for a few moments. "I'll be right there." She disconnected and put the phone down. She stood and smiled at him sadly. "I'll have to take a rain check on lunch and…that other thing. Float emergency."

Daniel groaned. He'd have that shower now. As cold as he could make it.

* * *

Daniel found his mother in her office at the family's restaurant, Luna el Sol. He'd grown up in this restaurant, and it was as comfortable to him as his bedroom. The bright colors always made him smile. He especially loved the huge bird cages that had originally contained live parrots and macaws. The birds had been annoying, and his father had replaced them with plush replicas from one of the LA Zoo's gift shops.

His mother glanced up at him, her eyes alight with humor as he entered. Her office was filled with elegant antique walnut furniture redolent of the southern California. Patio doors opened to a small atrium garden that contained wrought iron tables and chairs only used during good weather. The day, which had started out sunny, had changed, and now a hazy drizzle filled the late morning air. California needed the rain, so he didn't begrudge the weather.

"What's going on?' Daniel asked as he poured himself a mug of coffee from the tiny galley kitchen hidden behind louvered doors.

She gave him a piercing look. "Nothing's going on. What's wrong with you?"

He frowned. He hated when his mother just got to the point without the social lead-in. "Maybe I just came here to mooch breakfast."

She sat back and regarded him serenely. She was still a beautiful woman, not as slim as she'd been before seven pregnancies, but still slender with a long, narrow face, dark brown eyes and black hair threaded with gray pulled into a loose bun at the nape of her neck. She wore a black dress with a white shawl draped across her shoulders and pink pearls about her neck and in her ears. She'd been a backup singer to some of the best known rock groups of the seventies and eighties and still did some vocal work, but of late she'd tapered off to only a few jobs here and there. Nothing that took her away from home. Even with both of his parents working when he was young, Daniel had never felt deprived of his parents' company. Early in their marriage they'd decided that if one parent had to be gone, the other would be home. He was grateful for their presence in his life, then and now.

His mother looked at him. "I know you need to talk because Logan's already been here," she said with a knowing half smile.

Damn! Logan had beaten him to his own mother. He sat down on a chair and tried not to sigh in frustration.

"Why does this Greer Courtland have the two of you in such a Gordian knot?"

"Pulling out the fancy terms, are you?"

"I read a book once," his mother replied tartly. "Stop being a smart-ass and get to the point. I have work to do." She waved a hand over her desk and the piles of papers along with an overflowing in-box. "Have things progressed to the next stage already?"

The next stage? Was she talking about sex? "What are you asking me?" He never discussed sex with his mother. He discussed it with his brothers. She was his mother and wasn't supposed know about things like her children having sex. Yeah, she'd had seven children, but a part of him still wanted to think the stork had brought them, dropping them down the chimney like a Christmas present from Santa.

"From the look on your face, you and Greer spent the night together last night, didn't you?"

He squirmed. How could his mother make him feel like he was seven years old again with nothing more than a look and a partial smile? "I took her to Griffith Park last night and we looked at the stars." He didn't add that she'd invited him home afterward.

"Do I need to start looking for my mother-of-the-groom dress?" Grace teased.

"Mom, I'm your son. This is serious business and you're teasing me."

Grace Torres burst out laughing. "You look so serious. Love is supposed to be about exploration, fun and discovery. It's about finding what the two of you have with each other."

"I don't know if I'm in love." Yet a part of him thought he could be in love with Greer. From the first time he'd met her, she'd impressed him. "I've never been involved with a woman like this before. She confuses me. She's so different. She's not interested in…" He paused, thinking how best to say it.

"She's not interested in the trappings of your life." Grace leaned back in her chair, a look of amusement on her face. "You have finally met someone who isn't impressed with what you have, or what you can give her. She's looking for the man underneath all the illusion."

He'd never had to defend his lifestyle to a woman before. The women in his past had actually shared it; they'd understood the illusion as well as he did and asked nothing more of him. And yet every moment with Greer left him feeling like he had to do exactly that. He'd taken her to Griffith Park last night so she could see he was more than the sum total of his parts.

"So what do you want from me?" his mother asked gently.

He didn't know. He stared at his mother, trying to think, but his thoughts were a jumble that circled around and around Greer Courtland like she was the eye of a hurricane. "I want to know what to do next." He'd finally admitted what he needed. He didn't know how to be with Greer. Last night had been wonderful, and afterward at her house had been an experience he very much wanted to repeat.

Grace stood in a graceful motion. She came around the desk and cupped his face in her hands. "Be yourself, my dear. Just be yourself."

"Logan wants her, too." His one last fear appeared.

Grace bent over and kissed him on the forehead. "Logan just wants to irritate you."

"He's doing a fine job of it." Daniel didn't mean to sound bitter, but for the first time he had someone he truly wanted, and Logan was making things difficult.

"Only because you're letting him." Grace kissed him again.

Daniel stood and hugged his mother. "This thing with Logan never bothered me before."

"Because you feel different about Greer, and Logan is distracting you."

"Have you always been this wise?" She probably had been, but like most children, he tended to not listen to his parents. He and Nick had caused a lot of chaos during their teen years, and his mother had probably wanted to lock them both up in jail until they matured, but they'd all survived.

She smoothed a wayward curl back from his forehead. "I have seven children, I get a lot of practice. Now go out and get the girl. In fact, bring her to dinner tonight. Nina seems to like her. We'll introduce her to Brazilian cooking. I want to see how she eats."

"Why do you want to see how she eats?" Daniel was confused.

"Two words. *Dorothy Lambert*. Your old high school girlfriend you reconnected with after college."

He hadn't thought about Dorothy in years. But he did remember that at one point he'd thought she was the one. "Why?"

"She picked at her food and complained about the spiciness."

That really didn't explain anything for him. "Still not understanding, Mom."

Grace sighed and shook her head. "She was anorexic and when I tried to help her, she refused to have anything to do with me. I can't have a daughter-in-law who thinks I'm a busybody and has nothing nice to say about me."

"But you are a busybody," Daniel said with fondness. Dorothy had had her issues, but Daniel hadn't really seen them for what they were. After all, he'd thought he loved her. Eventually she dropped him for a smart-looking entertainment lawyer twenty years her senior, and he'd lost track of her.

His mother smacked him on the arm. "I admit I meddle, but I do it with love. Always with love."

He hugged her tightly. "Thanks, Mom."

"That's what moms are for."

Greer skirted around a float being jockeyed into position inside the huge tent set up in the Rose Bowl parking lot. She waited a moment for the float to be pushed into its spot and then headed down the aisle toward Chelsea, who stared up at Daniel's float.

"What's going on?"

Chelsea pointed at the rearmost butterfly, which was missing a wing. The wing lay crumpled on the ground next to the float. Not good, Greer thought.

"And the hydraulics were damaged, too."

"How did this happen?" It wasn't like the wing would just fall off. Greer knew her job.

"Unknown. I arrived this morning, and this is how I found it." Chelsea looked angry.

A lot could happen to damage a float, but this particular incident didn't really look like an accident. "Probably someone bumped into it while positioning their own float and didn't notice." Greer tried to sound soothing, but her own irritation was just beneath the surface. Respect for other floats was a big part of the business even as they competed for the trophies.

"I already called John, and he's on his way over to repair the hydraulic system. And I called the welder. He said he'd be here sometime today."

Greer simply nodded as she bent over the crumpled wing. She could redo it quickly enough, she thought. It was mostly composed of foam and aluminum screening. She went to work, smoothing out the screening, pulling it tight.

"Nothing ever goes smoothly," Chelsea said.

"What fun would that be?" Greer said with a light laugh. She sat cross-legged on the ground and started pulling the wing back into shape. Chelsea sat across from her and held one edge of the wing as Greer bent it. Little dings would hardly be noticed beneath the flowers.

"How was your date with Daniel last night?" Chelsea asked, her tone conversational with just a hint of curiosity.

"Fine," Greer said, her head bent as she concentrated on the wing.

"I can't imagine a date with Daniel would be just 'fine.' What did you do?"

Greer slanted her sister a fond look. She knew Chelsea was trying to act nonchalant, but her curiosity was slowly revealing itself. "He introduced me to his car collection, and then we piled into his truck—"

"He drives a truck? That seems so average."

"He has to have a way to get his telescope up the mountain."

Chelsea stared at her sister. "Telescope? That man constantly surprises me."

"Me, too. He set it up in a picnic area, and we spent hours watching the stars."

"That sounds…dull." Chelsea held on tight while Greer tugged. The foam was partially cracked. She would need glue for it and something to reinforce the break.

"Actually, it was fun," Greer replied.

"Even on a date, you're a stick-in-the-mud," Chelsea said with an exaggerated sigh.

"I am not," Greer objected.

Her sister grinned. "Big sister, you kind of are. You're with a man this gorgeous and what are you doing? Looking at little bits of light in the night sky."

"I took him home with me, " Greer said. "He spent the night." She sighed. And what a night it was. Just the memory sent tingles of heat across her skin.

Chelsea's eyes narrowed. "I don't believe you. You haven't had a boy-girl slumber party in years… decades."

"Decades? I'm not old enough to not have had sex in decades."

"Then years," Chelsea amended.

"Two at most. You're forgetting Roy." She'd dated him two years ago, and they'd had some pretty nice sleepovers.

"And he is best forgotten," Chelsea said.

"Why? I liked Roy."

"He liked Roy, too," Chelsea said.

Roy had been a male catalog model trying to leverage his way into commercials. He'd been pretty to look at, and while Chelsea had made no bones about the fact that she considered him shallow, he had been nice to Greer and made her feel desirable. Not that she wasn't, but her time between dates seemed to go on so long, she often started to think something was wrong with her. Chelsea had once told her she was too focused on her work and too particular about whom she wanted to date.

"What's Daniel like in bed?" Chelsea inquired with a gleam in her eye. "Was he fun?"

Greer grinned. "Mind your own business."

"See," Chelsea chortled, "you are a stick-in-the-mud. You never talk about your love life. All we get is, 'I'm seeing someone,' and we have to fill in the blanks.'"

"I think you talk too much about your love life…"

"And lack thereof," Chelsea said.

"…and that balances us out," Greer finished. She didn't want to say anything about the pending divorce. Chelsea was already sensitive about it. Like their parents, Chelsea had wanted a marriage that lasted. Unfortunately, her soon-to-be ex-husband hadn't gotten the memo. She was still smarting from the email she'd received from him one night saying he'd filed for divorce. The man hadn't even had the courage to tell her to her face.

John arrived, Chelsea jumped to her feet to consult with him on the hydraulics and Greer was left to finish straightening out the wing.

By the time Greer left the tent, she was ravenous. She'd missed lunch. While she walked to her car, she called Daniel to see if he was free for a late lunch. He agreed to meet her at his office, and she said she'd bring lunch.

As she drove, she replayed the conversation with her sister. She wasn't a stick-in-the-mud. She wasn't quite sure what she was. Discreet, maybe? She just didn't like her business on the street.

Daniel heard the door open, and he looked up from his laptop to find Greer standing in the doorway, watching him. "Hi. You made faster time than I thought."

She grinned at him. "You have a couple of minutes?"

Not really, but for her he'd make the time. "Do we have a float issue?"

She stepped inside his office and closed the door. "No."

He heard the lock on his door click. Interesting, he thought. She wore a black trench coat tightly belted at the waist. Was it raining today? He glanced out his window to see sunshine and clear skies. "What's up?"

"Chelsea said I'm a stick-in-the-mud."

"You are?"

"According to my sister, I have the sense of adventure of a rock." She put her purse and a large tote on his sofa.

"I'm not judging."

"Good, because I need you to help me with that."

"How?"

She untied the belt and let the trench coat slide from her body, leaving her in nothing but a red bra and panties. When he dragged his gaze to her eyes, she fluttered her lashes at him.

"Well, okay, then." He shut his laptop and moved it to the edge of his desk.

She came around and sat on his desk. Then she grabbed his tie and pulled him toward her. Before he could say anything, she leaned toward him and kissed him. There was nothing sweet or playful about this kiss. Her lips crushed his, and he could taste the hunger on her mouth and the sweetness of her breath. She thrust her tongue in his mouth and seemed to take what she wanted. Daniel felt his tie slide from his neck. As she unbuttoned his shirt and pulled it off, he unfastened her bra and slid the straps off her shoulders.

She pulled his head down, and he was only too happy to nuzzle her breast. Her skin was so soft and warm, he thought he'd die from wanting her. He could have done this forever. Quickly she helped him undress. For a second he felt a bit self-conscious about doing this in his office, but the second she got his pants around his ankles, he left that thought behind.

He grabbed her and led her around the desk, then lay down on the sofa and positioned her above him. He was ready, hard and erect. She moved over him, taking him inside her with a deliberate slowness that both tortured him and ignited him. Finally he was buried deep inside her. For a moment they didn't move.

"Make love to me." Her voice was soft and sultry and sent his blood rushing in his veins.

Greer buried her face in his neck, and he felt her lips on his skin.

He liked her. He wanted her. He needed her.

He gripped her behind and started directing her hips to rock against him. With each movement her breasts glided across his skin. He skimmed his hands up and down her supple back and cupped her butt cheeks, trying to control her movements, but she nipped him in the neck.

Greer increased the tempo of her thrusts, and he became lost in the moment as heat blazed inside him. Then his body ignited, and his orgasm built and built until he could no longer contain himself. Pleasure blinded him, and all he could feel was Greer shuddering, her muscles contracting around his penis, her breath coming in short, labored puffs, as she came with him.

In that moment, everything changed. He wasn't sure how, but he knew it did. They lay clasped in each other's arms for a few minutes, or maybe a few hours. Then she kissed him on the cheek and got up.

Greer quickly put on her bra, panties and shoes, then cinched the belt of her trench. "See you later." She waved and walked out his office door.

For a second, he was too stunned to react. Then he started laughing.

Greer didn't know what to expect when she walked into the Torres family restaurant. Her parents had eaten there and raved about the food. They'd even mentioned the aborted experiment with the birds, and Greer had laughed with them.

Bright colors greeted her as Daniel escorted her past the people waiting in line in front of the hostess stand and into the main dining room filled with the scents of so many foods, her nose couldn't separate them.

Daniel led the way across the dining room. Greer noticed a few faces turned to look at him, recognition in their eyes. Someone raised a phone and snapped a photo.

At the back of the restaurant, a private area was partitioned off the main dining room by planters containing green shrubs. The secluded area held two long tables and a sideboard that looked to Greer like a Victorian antique. The niches held dishes and glasses, and in the center a mirror reflected the cozy room. Upholstered chairs surrounded the tables, which were covered with bright orange tablecloths and colorful place settings. At a discreet distance from the table, a waitress stood.

At one table, Daniel's sister Nina sat with a man Greer assumed was her husband. Logan sat across from them. He and the other man pushed to their feet politely as she neared the table.

Daniel did the introductions. "You remember my sister Nina. This is Scott, her husband."

Scott was a tall, hard-looking man, and the expression he gave her had a directness to it that seemed to see into her soul. He held out a hand and Greer shook it. When he glanced at his wife, his gaze softened.

"Mom and Dad are in the back, putting the finishing touches on our meal," Nina explained after Greer sat down.

Greer found herself sandwiched between Logan and Daniel. The second Daniel seated himself, the waitress bent over to take her drink order unobtrusively. Greer asked for a glass of pinot noir, and Daniel ordered a bottle.

"So how does one become involved in float construction?" Nina asked. "Seeing all those floats really started me thinking." She selected a roll from a large basket in the center of the table.

"It's Pasadena. The Rose Parade is who we are and what we do." Greer smiled at Nina. "Look at you. You're all involved in some form of entertainment." Her mother had given her background on the Torres family.

Nina shrugged. "It's Los Angeles. What else are we going to do?"

"I could say the same about Pasadena. I love the pageantry, and I'm delighted to have a skill that is of use."

"Greer is a very talented artist," Daniel explained.

"That's really more a hobby," Greer replied.

"So she's shown you her etchings, has she?" Logan put in. He studied Greer with a tilt of his head. Daniel looked annoyed. Logan slapped Daniel on the back. "You go, bro."

"Did you just say something inappropriate about me?" Greer asked Logan.

"Logan is always inappropriate." Nina bit into her bread.

Logan grinned. "I work very hard at it."

She didn't like being under such a microscope. To cover up her discomfort, Greer reached for a piece of bread. It was cheesy and moist and tasted as delicious as it smelled. "This is very good."

"Pão de queijo," Daniel said. "Brazilian cheese bread." He glanced at Nina. "Do you know what we're having for dinner tonight?"

Nina nodded. *"Canja*, which is a soup," she explained to Greer, "then *churrasco de porco com queijo ralado*, an herby pork loin sprinkled with parmesan cheese, served with barbecued pineapple and rice, and for dessert we have *pudim de leite*, which is a pudding."

"Mom's been cooking all afternoon, hasn't she?" Daniel asked her.

"We have to take Greer through her paces," Nina said, reaching for another roll.

"You hold nothing back, do you?" Greer said.

"I've spent years dealing with Hollywood people in crisis mode. I've saved films, careers, reputations. I can't afford to be anything else but blunt."

"I appreciate that." Greer was generally direct, but she tried to be more subtle because she was selling a service and had to consider a client's needs and merge them with the practical aspects of float design.

"Nina's the family muscle," Daniel said. "When she was in first or second grade, she faced down a bully who was extorting the little kids for their lunch money. She made him give every penny back, and then she went to the principal and made sure it never happened again. And when I was accused of stealing a friend's wallet in high school, she searched out the person who did it and I was exonerated."

"So you're the one to have on my side," Greer said.

"I am." Nina nodded.

Just then, Daniel's parents swooped down. *Swoop* was the only word Greer could think of to describe the way Mrs. Torres kissed everyone, including her. Mr. Torres clapped the three men on the back with jovial humor and kissed Greer and Nina on the forehead. Behind them came two waiters. One carried a large covered soup tureen, and the other held a stack of bowls and a second basket of bread.

"Now," Mrs. Torres said grandly, "Manny and I are here, so the party can start." Her husband held her chair out for her, and she sat down at the head of the table with a huge smile on her face. Manny went around to the foot of the table and sat down.

Greer seized the opportunity to acknowledge her hosts. "Mr. and Mrs. Torres, thank you for inviting me to dinner."

"Mr. and Mrs. Torres were Manny's parents," said Daniel's mother. "I'm Grace, and he's Manny."

Logan leaned close to her ear. "We all just call them Mom and Dad."

Greer turned to look at him. "How did you get into the family?"

"Who doesn't want me?" Logan said.

Grace reached over and patted Logan's hand. "We took pity on the poor little rich boy."

"And I thank God every day," Logan said with a beaming smile at the older woman.

Greer figured there was a story somewhere in that statement, but she was too polite to ask. Her mother had drilled manners into her.

Grace took Scott's hand. "And our little family is growing."

Little? Greer hid a smile behind her napkin.

As the waiter served the first course, a heavenly aroma rose from the soup, which seemed to consist of carrots, tomatoes and rice with bits of chicken floating in it.

"Eat up," Grace said once everyone was served. "Nina, you're too skinny, and now you are eating for two."

"How wonderful," Greer said. "Congratulations."

"Thanks." Nina dipped her soup spoon and took a long breath of the steam rising from it.

Logan squeezed Greer's arm. "You could eat a little more, too. The other night at Craig's, you just pushed your food around on the plate and took only a couple of bites."

Greer simply smiled. She wasn't about to tell him that the night had made her so uncomfortable she'd had no appetite. "I have every intention of relishing each bite tonight."

Grace beamed in approval. "Most men like women with a little meat on their bones. Up until the Regency period, a woman with curves was considered desirable. It meant she had a husband who made good money, and she could live a life of leisure."

Manny laughed. "And when are you going to start living a life of leisure?"

"If I stayed home doing nothing, I'd probably burn the house down," Grace replied.

Manny grinned. "I'm not saying you should do nothing."

Greer leaned over to Daniel. "Your family is hilarious." Her own parents were more sedate, more serious, always thinking about the work that needed to be done and the next year's parade. They were loving parents, too, but in a more restrained way.

"It's a laugh riot around here," Daniel replied.

The soup was excellent, and under Grace's watchful eye, she finished it and even had a second cheesy roll. The waiter and waitress removed the bowls when they were finished and withdrew again.

Greer turned to Daniel. "Now do I have to take you home to dinner with my parents?"

"I've met your entire family, but only to discuss the float." Daniel saw that her wineglass was empty and refilled it.

Greer knew Daniel had originally met her father when he'd first decided to sponsor a float. Her dad had left them pretty much alone until his recent interest as the time got closer to the parade.

"That was business," Greer said. "People are different when there's wine on the table."

"I wish I'd hired your parents to create my float,"

Logan put in. "My design seems all right, but it doesn't sparkle."

"I've seen your float," Greer said. "It's going to look a lot different when all the decorations are done. I think you'll be surprised. And if you're still not happy, I've seen Sabrina Palmer rip a float apart and fix it in forty-eight hours."

"Has your company ever done that?" Daniel asked.

"More times than I care to count, and trust me, I didn't sleep for a week." The memories made Greer shiver. "That was the float that made me decide to major in structural engineering so that it doesn't happen again." She turned back to Logan. "Don't worry. You're in good hands."

The waitstaff returned with covered plates. As one waiter uncovered a plate, the other one delivered it, and in no time everyone had their entrées.

Grace instructed them to begin eating, keeping up the conversation without missing a beat. "The couple of years Manny and I helped sponsor a float, we were never disappointed in your family's work," she said.

"The Brazilian Mardi Gras–themed float you designed a few years ago was brilliant." Manny pointed at a photo on the wall. "It won the President's Trophy that year."

Greer loved that float. It was her first design after her graduation from Cal Poly Pomona.

Logan jostled her arm, and she looked at him to see an amused expression on his face. "I hear Daniel took you to see the constellations last night. I can do better than that. I have an invite to a party at Emerson James's house in Malibu tomorrow night. I can pick you up for an early dinner and—"

"Who is Emerson James?" Greer asked searching her brain for a reference. Nothing came to her.

"Never mind," Logan said, looking deflated. "But for your information, he's only been football's MVP the last two years running."

"Oh, a football player," Greer responded. "My dad follows soccer, but my sisters and I aren't really into sports. I did play volleyball in college, but just for fun." Rachel had played softball in high school, but Chelsea had been into more esoteric pursuits as president of the debate club at UCLA and a member of the chess club. Their desire to compete had been completely channeled into the family business.

"Then how about just dinner?" Logan didn't give up easily.

Greer looked at Daniel and found him watching her intently, his lips pressed together tightly, his shoulders stiff. The rivalry between the two men made her uneasy. She just didn't get it. "I'm afraid not," she told Logan quietly.

She felt Daniel relax next to her. Still, he leaned toward his friend to say, "Stop making Greer uncomfortable."

"I like the challenge." Logan looked defiant.

Grace patted Logan's arm gently. "Logan, that's enough. She has given you her answer." Her voice held a command, though gently put.

Logan bowed his head, but Greer had a feeling this wasn't over.

Chapter 6

Greer had been reluctant to part from Daniel, but every day was a workday from now until the parade. She needed to check out the welder's work on the wing and see if John had finished repairing the hydraulic system.

But first she had another job to do. The evening she'd spent watching the constellations with Daniel had given Greer an idea. The idea had germinated the last two days and blossomed while she was getting her breakfast this morning. Suddenly it all clicked in her mind, coming together with such completeness, her fingers itched to draw it out.

She walked into the reception area of Courtland Float Designs. Sadie, their Jill-of-all-office-chores, snickered at her.

"What's wrong?" Greer asked.

"You'll see," Sadie said in a mysterious tone just as the phone rang and she lifted it to her ear.

As Greer walked down the long hall to her office, Rachel peeled out of her office and fell into step with her.

"You must have had a really nice weekend." She drew out the word *really* as though it was fourteen syllables long.

"What do you mean?" Greer asked, suddenly curious. Rachel's remark, combined with Sadie's odd comment, told her something was going on.

Chelsea poked her head out of her office and grinned at Greer. She joined them.

"Why are you coming to my office with me?" Greer asked.

"We're having a meeting," Chelsea said.

Rachel grinned. "Yeah. A meeting."

Greer didn't like the way her sisters sounded. What was going on?

She flung open the door to her office and was almost blown backward by the intense fragrance of roses. She staggered against the doorjamb.

Every surface and half the floor were filled with roses. Dozens of roses in every color.

"You must have really made an impression on Daniel," Chelsea said slyly.

Greer stared at the roses. The riot of color made her head ache. This didn't sound like Daniel. He wasn't this flamboyant. She found a card dangling from a stem and opened the envelope.

Roses are red.
Roses are blue.
But they don't compete
With the beauty that's you.
—Logan Pierce

"What is this?" Chelsea grabbed the card. "Logan Pierce? I could have sworn these roses came from Daniel." She sounded so disappointed, Greer almost laughed.

"Not his style," Greer said.

"And it is Logan Pierce's style," Rachel said.

"How do you know about Logan Pierce's style?" Greer asked.

"I'm a fan," Rachel replied. "I watch his show."

"But you don't like sports," Greer said.

"I like to look at guys who play sports." Rachel's voice was defensive.

"What are you going to do?" Chelsea gestured at all the flowers.

"We'll get Dad's truck and take them over to the children's hospital. But first, I should call him and say thank you." Greer reached for her phone and walked back out into the hall. The scent of the roses was so overpowering, she was getting a headache. Rachel and Chelsea grinned at her and leaned against the wall.

"Go away," Greer said.

"Not a chance," Rachel said.

Greer dialed Logan's number. He'd flown back to New York the night before, so at least she didn't have to agree to a date with him as a way of thanking him. Fortunately, her call went to voice mail. "Thank you so much for the lovely flowers. They're beautiful. I appreciate them." After that succinct message, she disconnected the call.

She glanced back at her office. Too bad he hadn't sent them closer to Christmas. Chelsea could have recycled them onto a float. But this early, they would never last.

"Boy, did he get it wrong." Chelsea bent over a bouquet and sniffed. "But it was a worthy try."

"He should have opted for daisies," Rachel said.

"Cut him some slack," Greer said, feeling as though she needed to defend Logan but not understanding why.

"He's pretty to look at. I'll give him that," Chelsea put in. "All that blond hair and his muscular body. His football career may be over, but his football body is still kickin'."

Chelsea liked a man who looked good and was uncomplicated. After spending four years married to Mr. Faux-genius who spent all his time trying to impress people with his superior intelligence and make everyone else feel stupid, she needed uncomplicated. Logan would be perfect for her.

Rachel opened the door to the broom closet and pulled out a wheeled cart while Chelsea went to their father's office to get the truck keys. Rachel pushed the cart into Greer's office and started putting the vases on it. "Aren't Logan and Daniel really good friends?"

"They're best friends," Greer said as she grabbed

a vase and set it on the cart. "But they seem to enjoy competing over everything."

"How does that make you feel?"

"I find them both amusing."

"Apparently you've made your choice, since you're not sleeping with Logan," Chelsea said as she entered the office, the truck keys jingling in her hand. "How are things going?"

Heat flared across Greer's cheeks. "He doesn't think I'm a stick-in-the-mud." After their interlude in his office, if he had thought that, he didn't anymore.

Chelsea laughed. "Where are the two of you heading?"

"I like being with him, but I don't want anything more complicated than that, at least not right this moment." She loaded some more vases and instructed Chelsea to park the truck at the front door. "We're going to have to make several trips."

Chelsea trotted down the hall. Greer and Rachel finished filling the cart and pushed it down the hallway to the front door.

"That's quite a haul," their mother said from the doorway to her office.

"We're taking them to the children's hospital," Rachel explained.

"Don't do that. Children would rather have a stuffed animal. Take them over to the retirement community on Main. Where did they come from?"

"Logan Pierce is determined to sweep me off my feet," Greer said.

"I'd wish him good luck, though I know Daniel has already won."

"Logan is very likeable, too." She defended the man, because she couldn't admit her mother was right. It irked her that everyone in the world knew about her love life. She didn't even have secrets from her mother. She glanced at Rachel, who looked away, a guilty expression in her eyes. Rachel never could keep a secret, and their mother relentlessly exploited her susceptibility to parental pressure.

"Of course he is." Her mother turned back into her office with a tiny wave of her hand.

A stagehand placed two chairs on a ten-by-ten-foot square of carpet in the center aisle of the huge tent. Floats, arranged in long lines, filled the tent, while volunteers swarmed the area like an army of ants. The sounds of hammering, laughter and squealing hydraulics surrounded Daniel as he watched the film crew set up for the next segment.

"What are we doing?" his director asked.

"We're having a parade float safety drill." Daniel's brother Nick looked amused.

"What exactly does a float safety drill entail?" Nick's dance partner, Michelle, stood to one side of the float, staring up at it. She was a tall, willowy blonde with intense blue eyes and a creamy complexion that reminded Daniel of a woman he'd met on a trip to Ireland.

"I have no idea," Daniel replied. "For all I know, it could involve lifeboats. In case of flood."

One of the two cameramen snickered. "When I was filming *Titanic*, I ended up as an extra and died when the boat went down."

Daniel grinned. "Big surprise there. I promise, if anything happens, you'll be the first person I save. You always make me look good."

"Thanks, boss." The cameraman saluted Daniel and turned back to setting up his equipment.

Greer walked quickly down the aisle. Daniel's heart lurched at the sight of her. She looked so delectable in her skinny jeans, cable-knit sweater and knee-high boots.

"Sorry I'm late." Greer set a briefcase on the side of the float and opened it to pull out a folder. "Where shall I start?" She handed Daniel and Nick sets of stapled papers.

"I didn't know there were procedures for float safety." Nick glanced through the papers.

"Safety is no joke," she retorted. "People have given their lives to make floats safe."

Nick grinned at her. "You said that with a straight face."

"I know talks about safety can be boring. I'm trying to make this fun. So go with the spirit." Greer handed a set of papers to Nick's dancing partner, Michelle, who started flipping through them with a serious look on her face.

Greer started to explain where the fire extinguishers and the first aid kits were. "We try to be prepared for everything—earthquakes, fire, zombie invasion, alien apocalypse."

Nick shook his head. "Zombie invasion."

"It could happen," Greer said with a tiny twitch at the corners of her mouth.

Daniel wanted to laugh. She was good. No wonder his audience loved the segments he did with her.

"Don't forget *Sharknado*," the cameraman put in.

Greer pointed at him. "See. He understands. I can work with him."

"So, float lady," Nick drawled, "what do we do in case of a *Sharknado* event?"

"You're on your own. Just remember the sharks tend to come down headfirst, so stay away from their teeth."

Daniel grinned as she explained the safety harness. "The float only goes five miles an hour. What do we need a safety harness for?"

She held up two fingers. "Two words. *Law* and *suit*."

"That's three words, but one if you just say *lawsuit*."

She patted him on the cheek. "All right." She walked around the float, pointing out where people would be stationed. "As for Nick, you and your partner need to stay within the boundaries of your dance floor. The float is balanced, and all your weights are taken into account." She pointed at the dance floor already in place. "Stay on that square."

She walked around the float, pointing out where the driver would be. "In case of a fire or other catastrophe, don't just jump off the float. It is moving. The driver will come to a stop, and then you can exit the float. Does everyone know how to use a fire extinguisher?"

"Doesn't everybody?" Daniel said.

She glanced over her shoulder at him. "Not a former mayor of New York. It was not pretty."

"Does the float driver have a valid driver's license?" Michelle asked.

"Of course, and for that…" She pulled a mint tin out of her pocket and handed it to Michelle. "You get a prize."

"So that's a yes," Michelle said with a small bubble of nervous laughter.

"That's a yes."

Michelle held up the tin. "I will treasure this forever."

Chelsea nudged Michelle. "You should. She seldom gives away her mints."

Daniel grinned at Greer. He was enjoying himself. He hadn't expected Greer to make a topic as boring as safety into something fun. He knew his audience would enjoy it.

His phone rang, and he stepped away from the group to answer it.

"Hello, Daniel Torres," came a strange voice. "My name is Virginia Courtland, and I'm Greer's mother."

"Hello," he said in a cautious tone, wondering what Greer's mother wanted with him.

"How are you doing today?" she asked chattily.

"I'm good, Mrs. Courtland."

"Call me Virginia. I'm dying to meet you."

"You are?" Was this a good thing or not? He knew

his parents liked the Courtlands but didn't really socialize with them.

"Of course. I'm calling to invite you to dinner. My husband and I have a ton of leftovers from Thanksgiving, and I'm a wizard at leftovers. It's a tradition to find a hundred creative ways to consume them. Though I will admit, I'm not the adventurous cook your mother is."

"I'm sure you're amazing."

She chuckled. "You keep believing that. We'll see you tonight around six. I'm texting our address to your phone." She disconnected.

He saw Greer conversing with the cameraman. He sauntered over, wondering if her mother had called her with the same commands.

"I just talked to your mother," Daniel said, drawing her away from the cameraman.

"Really? What did my mother want?" She frowned.

"To invite me to dinner."

She looked shocked. "This is not good."

Surprised, he stared at her. "Are you ashamed of me?"

She put a hand on his arm. "Heavens, no. It means my parents are butting into my personal life and intend to check you out. Don't worry. They're harmless."

Daniel wasn't so sure. "Rule number one—fathers are never harmless where their daughters are concerned. Rule number two—mothers always have ulterior motives."

Her eyebrows rose. "My parents are pretty laid-back. This is a bold move on my mother's part."

"Bold move or not, it has the touch of a royal command with a sledgehammer attached."

She grinned. "Don't worry. You'll do fine. They're really pacifists. It's pretty interesting, though. I haven't gotten a royal command phone call. I have a feeling you are on your own."

A nervous twitch pulled at his eye. It was time to sink or swim.

Virginia and Roman Courtland lived in a three-story Victorian mansion a few blocks away from the Norton Simon Museum. A green lawn, shrubs and formal flower beds that rimmed the house, extending to the edges of the property. He pulled into a circular drive bordered by topiary in various shapes and surrounding a large fountain. As he parked his car, he noticed his was the only one. He didn't know what to expect.

He stepped out on the gravel drive to the sound of water trickling down a stone sculpture in the center of the fountain. Koi poked their heads up over the surface of the water to eye him as though they expected to be fed. He walked up the concrete steps to the veranda, wiping his suddenly sweaty palms on the sides of his pants, and rang the doorbell.

Virginia Courtland was a carbon copy of her daughter—pretty and fashionable. She smiled at him and gestured him into a foyer. "Come in, Daniel."

He entered the well-lit foyer, smiling nervously.

"You look even nicer in person than you do on TV," Virginia said with a wide smile. Her black hair was cropped into a stylish bob, and she wore black slacks and a cream-colored silk blouse with a red-and-cream scarf around her neck. Diamonds glittered in her ears and on a bracelet around one wrist.

She led him into a huge living room appointed with tasteful Arts and Crafts furnishings and Erté prints on the walls. He could see where Greer got her taste in vintage furniture. In front of a roaring fireplace, Roman Courtland stood, a glass of what looked like bourbon in his hand.

"Good to see you again," Roman said, stepping forward to shake his hand. "I had nothing to do with this. The dinner invite was my wife's idea."

Daniel shook his hand. "Good to see you again, too. I appreciate the invitation." His mother had drilled manners into him.

"Can I get you something to drink?" Roman headed to a discreetly placed bar in one corner of the room. "I have bourbon, wine, vodka…"

He wanted to order one of everything, but he didn't think that would make a good impression on her parents. "I'll take a glass of white wine. Riesling, if possible."

"In my house, anything is possible," Roman said with a hearty laugh. He opened a small undercounter refrigerator and set a bottle of wine on the counter. He opened it expertly and poured it into a wineglass that caught the firelight and reflected a rainbow of colors. Real crystal, Daniel thought.

"Sit down," Virginia ordered. "Tell me about yourself."

"As an interviewer," he said, "I always find it more interesting to ask a direct question rather than something vague."

Virginia smiled sweetly at him. "As a mother, I prefer a more vague question because it gives a person more of a chance to trip up."

Daniel took a gulp of wine. "Nicely played, Virginia."

She grinned delightedly and sat back on the sofa, picking up her own glass of a red wine and taking a sip. She indicated a tray of appetizers. "Try one, please."

He looked around. "I was kind of expecting Greer."

"I'm sure she'll show up later," Virginia said with a wave of one hand.

Daniel crossed one leg over the other and smiled, relaxing a bit, knowing she would be coming soon. "So, what do you want to know? You can either ask questions you already know the answers to in order to establish a baseline, or jump off a cliff and ask the questions you really want to know the answers to."

Virginia burst out laughing. "This is going to be fun." She clapped her hands. "We were beginning to despair. Greer hasn't had a date in over two years."

"Do you think that's because she just chooses not to go out, or because no one has asked her out?" Daniel asked.

"Because she chooses not to go," Roman answered. He sat down next to his wife and popped a tiny quiche into his mouth. "Which is why we are so curious about you."

Daniel delayed answering as he looked over the selection of appetizers on the tray. He saw dumplings, tiny quiches, edamame, green chips of some type and three different dips. If his mother had been in charge, the appetizer tray would have had a hundred selections and would probably have substituted for a meal.

"I'm not bragging," Daniel said. "I have an interesting job and good communication skills. I own my own home free and clear, and I like cars and astronomy."

Virginia's eyebrows rose. "Astronomy. That's an unusual hobby that we'll give you points for."

"Thank you."

"What are your intentions toward our daughter?" Roman asked.

How to answer that one? He couldn't tell them he was sleeping with their daughter and wanted to keep sleeping with her. What parent wanted to hear that? "We're still in the exploration stage." Where did he want the relationship to go? Greer was different from any other woman he'd known. With her he wanted to go slowly because he didn't want to rush her. He wanted to build something...permanent. Yes, the idea of permanence with Greer sounded right.

"That's an interesting answer," Virginia said.

Daniel took a deep breath. "That's the only answer you're going to get." He could understand parents wanting to protect their children, but Greer wasn't a child. She was a grown woman, and on some level, their relationship was none of anybody's business. Well, maybe his mom's, since she knew everybody's business anyway.

The front door opened and a draft of cold air swirled into the living room. Greer appeared in the doorway, removing a scarf from her neck and unbuttoning her coat.

"Good evening, parental units," Greer said. She draped her coat over a chair and advanced into the room.

"Darling," Virginia said. "I knew you'd be here. It's your favorite leftover night."

Greer rubbed her hands together. "Oh good, turkey and dumplings. I'm starved. Dad, I'd love a glass of chardonnay if you have a bottle open. Otherwise just whatever you have."

"Riesling?"

"That'll work." Greer advanced into the room and bent to kiss Daniel on the cheek. Her lips were cool.

"Thank you for rescuing me," he replied.

Her father handed a glass of Riesling to her, and she sat down on the chair next to Daniel. "Mom. Dad. Just so you know, the two of you and I will be having words about this situation."

Roman pointed at his wife. "She made me do it."

"Mom," Greer said, her eyes narrowing, "we've had this conversation before. You've done this to Rachel and Chelsea but never to me. Daniel is off-limits."

"You misunderstand," her mother said.

"No, I don't." She took Daniel's hand. "We're

going to eat turkey and dumplings. Then I'm going to be angry at you both."

"I'm glad to know you have priorities."

"Food always comes first." She dragged him to his feet. "Let's eat."

When Chelsea suggested lunch away from the float site, Greer eagerly accepted. She needed to get away from the chaos of hundreds of volunteers laughing and talking, hammering, last-minute welding and the overpowering scent of flowers. Unfortunately, Rachel couldn't make it. She had a meeting with their tax accountant.

Their favorite restaurant was a small diner just off Colorado Boulevard. Since the day was warm and pleasant, Greer and Chelsea chose to sit outside on the sidewalk patio. Old-town Pasadena was crazy busy. Christmas shoppers hurried from store to store, laden with packages. Christmas music blasted from hidden speakers. Every store and lamppost was hung with Christmas lights and wreaths, and jolly Santas stood on street corners ringing their bells, red pots waiting for donations.

Greer studied the menu while Chelsea people-watched.

"Why do you do that?" Chelsea asked.

"Do what?" Greer glanced up.

"You always read the menu even though you order the exact same thing every time."

"Because I'm waiting for you to make up your mind."

Chelsea was a more adventurous eater than Greer. She would have been the first to eat chocolate-covered insects if they were on the menu.

"Touché." Chelsea went back to people-watching. "Your brutal honesty makes you the best sister ever."

"I know," Greer said with a chuckle.

After the waitress took their drink order, Chelsea asked, "How did it go with Mom and Dad last night?"

"Mom and Dad skewering my date was…interesting. Though I have to admit, it could have been more brutal." Her parents seemed to approve of Daniel. And Daniel had responded to their third degree with gentlemanly politeness. His parents had certainly raised him right.

"They like Daniel," Chelsea said. "They're brutal only with people they don't like."

The waitress returned with their sodas, and they ordered salads for lunch. Greer's favorite was bacon-ranch salad with cheddar cheese sprinkled on top and as much bacon as the chef could load on the greens. Chelsea decided on a quinoa salad with mangoes.

"I knew they would like him," Greer replied, though a touch of anxiety had stayed with her long after she and Daniel had left for their own homes.

"They didn't like my soon-to-be ex-husband," Chelsea said sadly. "I should have listened."

"We all make mistakes," Greer commiserated. She'd often thought Chelsea's desire to marry Christopher had been a rebellion against their parents' disapproval.

"Mom and Dad are happy because you're seeing somebody. They think you're too solemn."

Greer felt a silly grin spread across her face. "I'm happy I'm seeing somebody, too."

"How serious are the two of you?"

Greer paused to think about her answer. "Serious enough." Just looking at Daniel made her heart flutter and her pulse pound. And what he did to her body— Maybe that wasn't the right thing to think about with her too-observant sister.

Chelsea's eyes narrowed. "You're being evasive. Don't be. I'm living vicariously through your love life."

"I really like Daniel, but I don't know where we're heading. I'm enjoying the moment." Her boldness in going to his office and seducing him almost made her blush. She'd never done anything so daring before. Though she had to admit the look of pleasure on his face made her want to repeat the action.

Chelsea rummaged through her purse. "So is the readership of the *Celebrity Buzz*." She held up a tab-loid magazine.

Greer gasped. Her photo was plastered across the front. "What is this?" She grabbed the magazine.

"Came out this morning. Saw it while I was stand-ing in line at the grocery store."

Across the top was a photo of her and Daniel eating at his parents' restaurant. In the photo, she was look-ing adoringly at him, and his own gaze was heated as he eyed her. Over the photo was the headline For-mer Beauty Queen Meets Daniel Torres's Family. Beneath the headline was the subheading "Is this a serious romance for one of Hollywood's most eligible bachelors?"

"No. No. No. No. No." Greer opened the magazine, paging through it to find the story. The article, plastered with more photos of her and Daniel laughing and talking with his parents, Nina Russell and her husband, and Logan, read like a horror novel. "What am I supposed to do about this?"

Chelsea shrugged. "The story is not unflattering. You do look fabulous in the photos."

Greer gazed in shock at the page. "Why is this important?" she asked. "The world's in crisis and all this rag can think of is who Daniel is dating?" The effrontery of the idiots who wrote for this magazine! Could she sue them? Seeing her face plastered across the pages left a hollow, angry feeling in her.

Chelsea leaned forward, resting her elbows on the table. "I will be the first to tell you, I love me some good celebrity gossip, but wow, when my own sister is under the microscope, everything is different."

Greer read the short article quickly. After all, the sensational photos already told most of the story. "This feels so judgmental." For some reason the *Celebrity Buzz* was more interested in condemning her for stealing Daniel from some unnamed starlet. She hadn't stolen him. What was their problem?

"I followed the comments on the internet, and most of them are very nice, though. Except for this one guy who said your earlobes are fat."

Greer touched her ears. "My earlobes are fat? Can earlobes be fat? What a silly comment to make."

"He probably wanted to say something really nasty but couldn't find anything, so he settled for earlobe fat. Your ears are shaped like Grandma DeeDee's."

"What does that mean?" Greer asked.

"Grandma DeeDee had thick earlobes and always had trouble keeping her earrings on."

Greer simply frowned. "I don't have trouble with my earrings." She touched her ears again. Her dangling red poinsettia earrings were just where they were supposed to be. "They couldn't say I'm an award-winning float designer? Why a former beauty queen with chubby ears? That doesn't define me." Her anger turned to fury, and she felt like hitting something. How could this magazine so distort the truth?

"*Former beauty queen* is sexier than *float designer*." Chelsea's voice was matter-of-fact.

The waitress brought their salads, and for a few moments they were silent as they ate. A shadow fell across them, and Chelsea looked up.

"Can I join you?" Logan Pierce pulled a chair over from a vacant table and sat down.

"I guess so," Greer said. She really wanted to say no. "When did you get back from New York?"

"Last night." He studied her, his gaze lingering on her ears. "I don't think your earlobes are fat."

Greer wanted to punch him. "You read the article."

"Of course I read it. Half the fun of being a celebrity is reading the crap they write about you and following the comments on the internet."

A couple of teenage girls walked by, their heads turning. At first Greer thought they were admiring

Logan, but they whipped out their cameras and took a photo of her. She wanted to scream *go away.*

Chelsea started to giggled. "Next week I think you're going to find a photo of you and Logan on the front of the *Celebrity Buzz* with the headline Love Triangle."

"Why don't you date my sister so she can go through this misery, too?" Greer suggested.

Logan laughed.

"That is really a loaded question," Chelsea said. "If he says no, I might feel insulted. If he says yes, do you really expect him to date me?"

Logan gave Chelsea an admiring look. "Dating your sister wouldn't be a hardship."

"I should think not," Chelsea said, "though I really don't want my photo plastered all over next week's tabloids, nor do I want comments about my earlobes."

The waitress appeared with a menu for Logan, who ordered a drink and a sandwich.

"In my opinion," Logan said to Chelsea, "your earlobes are flawless."

"You can dish it, can't you?" Chelsea fluttered her eyelashes at Logan. "No wonder Greer chose Daniel over you."

He sat back, one hand over his heart, pretend hurt on his face. "You are brutal." He turned back to Greer. "I'm not giving up."

"I'm not sure what to say to you." Greer wanted to stuff her bread stick in her mouth to keep her comments unsaid. "So, what are you doing in town?"

"Daniel's doing a segment on my float tomorrow."

The waitress brought his mug of coffee, and Logan took a sip.

"*Your* float?" Greer said.

Logan nodded. "Bottom line, this rivalry we manufacture each year is for charity. We pony up for each other's charity, and so does our audience."

Chelsea finished her salad and pushed the bowl away. "So, this whole competition thing is not about your egos, but about charity."

Logan grinned. "Oh, we have egos, but most of it's for show. Mix in an audience with those egos and we've produced entertainment." He held out his hands. "Ta-da."

Greer couldn't help thinking she liked Logan. If he were just a little less pushy, she might enjoy being with him as much as she did being with Daniel. "I haven't figured out if that's brilliant or sad."

"Daniel and I have been friends since high school. We both know just how far we can push each other without drawing blood. Our audiences like that we choose oddball things. One year we sponsored a curling match between our two studios. Donations to the little-known US Olympic curling team tripled that year. And when they won the gold medal, interest was really revived in the sport."

Greer had no idea what curling was, and the fact that an Olympic team existed surprised her.

The waitress came back with Logan's sandwich. As he took a bite, Greer looked out onto the busy sidewalk. She noticed a photographer at the end of the block, his huge camera pointed at Logan.

"Is that a paparazzo?" She nodded at the man. He was short and stout with a comb-over that flapped in the slight breeze.

"Yep, that's Charlie," Logan said after a quick glance over his shoulder.

"Can he get a decent photo from there?" Chelsea asked. She pretended to pose and wriggled her fingers at the photographer.

"I have an injunction against him. He has to stay a minimum of a hundred feet away. He broke into my condo a few months ago to take photos of where I live. Thank God the maid had come the day before. I'd forgotten my phone and walked back in just as he was taking photos of my underwear drawer."

"Gross," Chelsea exclaimed.

"I hope he stays out of my house and my underwear drawer." Greer frowned at the photographer. She knew she wasn't going to enjoy being the target of their cameras.

"Get security, if you don't have any, and buy good locks." Logan frowned at the man.

"How do you stand living in a fishbowl?" Greer asked.

"You make a game out of it."

Greer shuddered. She didn't think she would ever get used to being followed by photographers day and night, forever intruding in her life.

The waitress returned with their checks, and Logan grabbed them. "My treat, ladies. I'm glad I ran into you. Otherwise I would have been eating by myself."

"We've got to get back to work." Greer pushed back from the table and stood. "Thank you for lunch. And thank you for the roses. You sent so many, I shared them with the folks in the retirement community down the block from my office."

"Did you at least keep one?"

"Of course," Greer said. "I kept one vase." She glanced at her watch. "We really have to get back."

"How about dinner Friday?"

She paused, then shook her head. "Sorry, I already have a commitment."

"With Daniel?"

"Maybe." She threaded her way around the patio tables and stopped to wave at Logan, who sat at the table finishing his sandwich. Chelsea pushed her through an opening in the short fence that surrounded the sidewalk patio. He looked lonely sitting by himself, and Greer was half tempted to go back. She would have, but she had a meeting with the volunteers who would be helping with Daniel's float.

Logan smiled at Greer, gave her a small wave and turned back to his lunch.

Chapter 7

Logan's float celebrated triumph over adversity as a celebration of life. He'd kept his design simple, with a bank of storm clouds at the front of the float leading to a brilliant rainbow in the rear. Along both sides of the float were the words After the Storm. Officials from the American Red Cross populated his float, wearing uniforms from different eras, from modern to vintage. Across the front of the float was the word HOPE. Beneath the storm clouds were devastated buildings, and beneath the rainbow were the same buildings rebuilt. The design was both poignant and beautiful.

On the side of the float, which was still in skeleton format, Logan sat in a director's chair next to Daniel, who held up the artist's drawing of the finished float.

Greer stood off to the side with a small audience of volunteers, observing the segment for Daniel's show. She couldn't help but see the easy camaraderie between the two men.

The cameraman panned along the edge of the skeletal float and back to Logan's face as he explained why he'd decided on this design.

"One of my staff lost her house to Hurricane Sandy, and she commented that seeing the Red Cross setting up food lines and handing out blankets at the different shelters gave her hope," Logan said. "That's what I wanted to convey with my float. Hope. Celebrating in the aftermath of disaster is all about hope and the fact that life goes on."

"That's a noble thought," Daniel said, a glimmer in his eye. "But how are you going to feel after you lose the Sweepstakes Trophy?"

"I'm not going to lose," Logan said, his voice lightly teasing. "After all, I'm on a streak, and I see no end in sight."

Greer found herself clapping with the rest of the audience.

"Good." Daniel said. "Let your confidence soar, because when you plunge to earth after you lose the trophy to me, my victory will be so much sweeter."

"You always were a poor loser," Logan replied with a chuckle.

Daniel burst out laughing. "And you're a poor winner."

Logan shook his head. "Is there such a thing as a poor winner?"

"Of course—a winner who gloats."

"I never gloat."

"Yes, you do." Daniel smiled directly into the camera. "If you go to YouTube, you can see the Logan Pierce Heisman Trophy dance. That is gloating *and* embarrassing."

Logan laughed and faced the camera. "And I remember you doing the Sugar Bowl Samba."

"We won that game," Daniel put in, defending his college alma mater.

"Yes, and we all witnessed your end-zone demonstration." Logan leaned toward the camera. "And that would also be on YouTube."

Again the audience started clapping. Greer was fascinated by the two men. Their easy friendship made her a little envious. She'd had friends go in and out of her life, but the most consistent relationships she'd had were with her sisters.

A third man walked onto the makeshift stage and took a seat. Brian Kellerman from Associated Float Design was a short, round man with a jolly face that masked his competitive nature. He looked like Santa Claus and made the most of the similarity by growing a snow-white beard. Brian had once worked for Greer's father and learned everything he needed to know in order to strike out on his own and become a main competitor of Courtland Floats and Greer's nemesis. He was a man who liked to gloat. He might have cultivated his Santa Claus look, but Greer's father called him the Grinch.

"This is a winner," Brian said with an expansive

gesture to the structure behind him. "My floats have won thirty-one trophies over the last ten years." His gaze flashed over Greer as he bragged. She was unimpressed. She trumped his thirty-one trophies with the seventy-four her family had won over twenty years in the business.

Daniel glanced at Greer, and she could see by the expression on his face that he thought Brian was an arrogant ass, too.

"This one," Brian said, half turning to the float behind him, "is my best one yet. I have every confidence we will win the Sweepstakes Trophy again this year."

Daniel smirked. "I think I have a pretty good float to offer as competition."

Brian dismissed Daniel's comment with a shrug.

Logan's float was sentimental, it told a story and it was beautiful—or would be beautiful once flowers adorned it. Greer could admire it, but the judges had their own way of looking at a float, and it didn't always coincide with the designer's vision.

Brian leaned toward the camera, a pleasant smile on his face. "Greer Courtland is an amazing conceptual artist, but I'm brilliant."

"I see," Daniel said, his voice neutral.

Greer shook her head. She heard the same nonsense from Brian every year. One thing her father always said about Brian was that he was a lavish creative force, but he didn't always understand the mechanics needed to make a float work properly. Many of his designs had to be scaled back to become reality. Fortunately for Brian, he had a good partner in his wife, who kept him in check. In fact, Greer was surprised Petra wasn't here. She was normally the spokesperson for the company.

"How do you like working with Logan?" Daniel asked, his voice polite.

"He has good ideas."

Greer caught Logan's eye roll. Obviously Logan was not an admirer of Brian, either.

"This is hilarious." Chelsea nudged Greer. "Brian never gets tired of listening to himself."

"Unlike the rest of us," Greer half whispered. When Brian got nasty, everybody needed to get out of his way. She figured he'd control himself while on national TV. "It's a beautiful design and perfectly mirrors the parade theme."

"So does Daniel's float."

"Daniel's float is fun. And that's okay. Life should contain humor and whimsy." And what better symbolism than the monarch butterfly from caterpillar to winged beauty?

When the interview ended, Daniel announced a commercial break and wandered over to Greer. "So, what are my chances of winning that trophy?"

"Yours is a good float. But the judges have the final say. Too bad it's not a personality contest, because I'd win hands down."

Daniel laughed. "No kidding. How about dinner tonight?"

"I'm in. Why don't you come to my house and I'll cook."

"Sounds like a date."

"Seven?"

He nodded and wandered back toward the temporary set.

Before Greer could return to work, a copy of the tabloid with her and Daniel's photo was shoved in front of her face.

"Can I get an autograph?" Brian asked.

"Of course. I'd be delighted. Do you have a pen?"

Brian glared at her. "Sleeping with your client, are you?"

"I have incredibly good taste."

His eyes narrowed. Before he could say something else, Chelsea rescued her. "We have to get back to work, Brian. See ya." She dragged Greer away.

"Thank you for that," Greer whispered.

"My pleasure."

Greer took one last look around her living room. Everything was in order. She wasn't the neatest person in the world, but neither was she a slob. The dogs waited expectantly at her feet. The cat lay across a pillow on a chair she'd long ago claimed as hers. Everything had been dusted and tidied in a whirlwind of activity the moment she walked in the door. Her Stickley sofa and chair gleamed with leather cleaner, and the faint scent of vanilla wafted through the house from the candle she'd lit. The ambiance was perfect.

When she heard a knock, Greer opened the front door and stood aside for Daniel to enter. He stepped inside and presented her with a bouquet of daisies and a bottle of white wine. Immediately the dogs surrounded him, sniffing the bottoms of his jeans and looking up with the pitiful expressions on their faces that said *pet me.* Daniel obliged.

"Lovely," she said. "Daisies are my favorite flower."

"You never did strike me as a rose kind of girl, even if you were Rose Queen. Besides, just to be certain, I called Chelsea."

Great. Chelsea was probably right this moment sharing with Rachel, who would share with their mother, that Greer was entertaining Daniel with a home-cooked dinner.

Daniel stood up from petting the dogs and looked at her. "How about that segment today? I couldn't help but detect some tension between you and Brian Kellerman."

"That's a long story." Greer led him into her cheerful blue-and-white kitchen and rummaged for a vase while he stood at the patio door, gazing out at the garden, which looked a little barren in December except for a few hardy blooms on her plumeria plants. She found a vase and arranged the daisies in it, setting it in the center of the kitchen table, which she'd already set.

He leaned against the door and crossed his ankles in a casual pose. "I have time."

"My dad hired Brian when I was around ten. He looks harmless, but he isn't. When I was sixteen, my dad fired him. I found out later that Brian had decided to start his own company and was trying to steal my dad's clients. Brian was really angry, even though he's the one who was in the wrong. He talked trash about my family to the parade board of directors. Fortunately for us, my dad's reputation was such that Brian's accusations didn't take hold."

"This parade stuff is serious business, isn't it?" Daniel said.

"Pasadena has made the parade a way of life. A lot of money is on the table. A small float can cost upwards of $250,000 to $300,000. A large float with all the bells and whistles can cost three-quarters of a million dollars. And each parade contains around sixty floats. So do the math. In the float community, everybody knows everybody." She opened the wine and poured a glass, then checked the oven to see if the chicken was finally cooked. She hadn't cooked for herself in so long, she'd almost forgotten how to turn on the oven. "Sometimes the right word in the wrong ear can ruin somebody's career. I'm lucky. My parents made it a point of maintaining a high level of ethical behavior."

"My parents do have a high opinion of yours."

"Nice to know."

"So, how do you like having your photo plastered all over the tabloids?"

"I now know I have fat earlobes."

Daniel looked confused. "What?"

"According to one man on the internet, my earlobes are fat."

"Please don't read the comments. I never read them."

"Sorry. The comment is courtesy of my sister, and she took great delight in sharing it with me."

"Does your sister like you?"

"Of course she does, but you have sisters. You know a sister never passes up a chance to take you down a peg."

Daniel laughed. "That I get. Nina can't resist sending me a copy of any magazine I'm in. She's the queen of spin."

"I figured that out when we had dinner with her and your parents. Don't you have another sister?"

"Lola. She's a musical genius. Right now she's scoring a movie, and I haven't seen her in weeks. When she's working, she buries herself in her house in Venice Beach and doesn't come up for air until she's finished. My mother goes over twice a week to force her to take a break and eat. Otherwise she'd work until she exhausts herself."

"I can relate to that," Greer said, "When the theme for the next parade is announced, I go into deep design mode. I barely get out of my pajamas because it would take too much time to dress." She was usually up to her ears in adjusting designs she'd already drawn and created new ones from scratch.

"How do you compete against yourself?"

"Every client wants something different. They all get equal love. I have no favorites among my children."

"I was hoping my float might be your favorite."

She shook her head. "Nope."

"Am I your favorite something?"

"You're my favorite talk-show host."

He grinned and shook his head. "I have to tell you, Greer, you're good at keeping me and my ego in check."

"My job here is done, then." She smiled back. "Come on, let's eat dinner. I'm not a great cook like your parents are, but I know my way around the kitchen."

"Can't wait."

She served dinner—oven-fried chicken, asparagus wrapped in bacon and garlic potatoes. She lit candles on the table and lowered the overhead lights to a gentle dimness. As they ate, a comfortable silence fell over them, and Greer was loath to see the end. In the candlelight, she studied Daniel.

"About the tabloid article," Daniel said. "I feel like I should apologize."

That was sweet. He was such a gentleman. "I'll admit," she said, "I was both shocked and amused. I wanted to die from the shock at being the object of such scurrilous gossip, and I wanted to laugh at the hilarity of it all because the story was so silly. The fact that some man said I had fat earlobes made me feel like I didn't have the right to show my face to the world."

"Welcome to my life. Fortunately, another scandal will push us off the front cover and take our place. The best advice I ever received was just to ignore it. So many of the stories are so far from the truth, I can't help but laugh at times. There was a story once that

Logan brushed his teeth every morning with Johnnie Walker."

"Black or red?"

"Blue. Logan wasn't about to use the cheap stuff on his teeth."

She laughed. "I can't help but wonder why people buy these tabloid magazines."

Daniel paused, his head tilted to one side while he thought. "People who make a lot of money are always under scrutiny. The general population likes to know that celebrities can make mistakes and takes great pleasure in seeing them make those mistakes. And let's face it—some celebrities are just plain stupid. Some welcome the attention because it either feeds their egos or helps promote them. Nina says publicity is publicity, good or bad."

"If I'm going to be the object of such attention, then I want it to be good attention for my parents' company, not bad attention on my earlobes."

Daniel burst out laughing. "Will you stop? Your earlobes are fine. They're beautiful and I love them."

She touched her ears. "You love my earlobes!"

"They have character and spunk."

That was the coolest thing a man had ever said to her. Not that she was going to let it go without commentary. "So now I have fat, sassy earlobes."

"With character. Own them," Daniel said.

"This is the silliest conversation I think I've ever had."

"I think it's hilarious," Daniel said. "But can we move on to something else—like us?"

They'd finished the main course. As Daniel cleared the table, she brought out the crème brûlée, which was the only dessert she could do well.

"What about us?" she finally asked.

"I like you. In fact, I like you a lot."

His words were like a spark that lit a fire in her body.

"I like seeing you," Daniel continued. "I like the way you think. I like being with you."

Greer felt the heat burn a path to her feminine parts. Just being around Daniel made her want to run her hands over his chest and arms. She loved the way he felt lying next to her in bed, his skin hot against hers. Right now she wanted to feel that again. She put the thought on hold so she could reply.

"I like you, too. I like that you have a public face and a private face and you know how to integrate them. I like that you're not impressed by your celebrity. And I like that you're kind and generous." She looked into his eyes, seeing the amber color flare to life in the brown depths. She was afraid to ask her question, but she needed to know the answer. "Where do we go from here?"

He studied her for a moment before answering. "I think we need to relax, play it by ear, let things happen and not worry about the direction. What happens, happens."

Greer opened her mouth to concur, but instead a yawn came out. She clapped a hand over her mouth but couldn't stop the next one. "Sorry."

He grinned at her and stood. "I think that's my cue."

"Sorry," she apologized again. "Today was a long one, and it's going to get more hectic next week. And the day after Christmas I have to hit the ground running until all the floats are completely decorated."

He kissed her gently, his lips soft against hers. "I have to be at the studio by four a.m. tomorrow, so it's an early night for both of us."

She walked him to the door, reluctantly. She wanted him to stay, but she couldn't seem to keep her eyes open. She watched him walk down the brick sidewalk leading to the driveway. He waved once, got into his Mercedes and backed out. She closed the front door and leaned against it. Her dogs sniffed at her feet for a moment before heading back to the kitchen. A second later, she heard the doggie door flap open and closed as they scrambled through.

She cleaned the kitchen and headed to her lonely bed, all the while wondering where she was heading with Daniel Torres.

Greer put her hands over her ears and let out a moan. "I can't listen to any more."

Rachel pulled her hands down as Chelsea continued to read.

"'Sources close to us say this is one explosive love triangle. Logan Pierce and Daniel Torres are in competition for former beauty queen—'"

"'Former beauty queen'!" Greer exploded. "Like I haven't moved on with my life or something."

Chelsea continued, ignoring the interruption. "'—former beauty queen Greer Courtland of Courtland Float Designs.'" Having completed the sentence, she looked up at Greer. "Be quiet. You're taking all the fun out of this for me." She looked back down at the tabloid and continued to read. "'Greer, seen having lunch with Logan Pierce, seems to be on intimate terms with the hunky former football player. Are wedding bells in the air for either of them?'"

"What do you mean, 'intimate terms'? You were there and you're not even mentioned."

"You are N-F-A-A."

"What does that mean?" Greer eyed her sister.

"No fun at all."

"This is my life being dissected in the tabloids."

"And it's finally interesting," Rachel put in with a giggle.

Greer covered her face with her hands, feeling the heat emanating from her cheeks. The embarrassment of this continued scrutiny left her at the mercy of her family's weird sense of humor. Her father chortled every time he saw her, and her mother couldn't stop laughing. They weren't the ones under the microscope. Greer felt like a train wreck waiting to happen.

Logan peeked into her office. "Hey, Greer."

"Go away," she half screamed. "Go away. I don't want to be seen with you."

He stepped into her office, a small box with a red bow in one hand. "I'm not going away."

"Just stay away from me."

Logan took the magazine from Chelsea and

glanced at it. "Hey, don't take it so personally. Though I have to say, I haven't had this much fun since I dated Anya Baslov."

"Who is Anya Baslov?" Chelsea asked.

"Minor Russian tennis player. Great backhand, gorgeous legs, but not much going on between her ears."

"What does that say about you?" Rachel asked him.

"That I'm shallow, and I accept that. But the fact that I want to date Greer means I'm a man of substance."

"Greer the former beauty queen," Chelsea teased.

Greer growled deep in her throat. "Chelsea, Rachel, leave." She stood and pointed at the door.

Her sisters left, Chelsea laughing delightedly and Rachel giggling.

Logan closed the door. "Listen, I'm going to give you some advice about tabloid stories. First of all, they write crap hoping they'll get a reaction from you that will escalate into an even bigger pile of crap. Female stars have been pregnant so many times, they're solely responsible for the world's population explosion. At any moment the hottest starlet is desperate for a baby, she lives in fear of being pregnant, she's expecting quadruplets and she's moving to Vermont for the rest of her life. Don't get me wrong—there are celebrities out there who have their own brand of crazy, but they're smart enough to have a media team whose sole purpose is to cover it all up."

"Do you have crazy?"

"I don't have time for crazy. I like my job, and I'm always looking for interesting things to keep my audience coming back for more. Just ignore it. Trust me. Something else will come along in a week and you'll be old news."

"Promise?"

"Maybe this will make you feel better. This is an early Christmas present and an I'm-sorry present." He held out the small box to her.

"Sorry for what?"

"Sorry that you got caught between Daniel and me and our competition."

She took the box and shook it cautiously. "What's inside?"

"Open the box and find out."

She carefully undid the bow and opened the box. A hoop earring with a tiny row of diamonds set in platinum winked at her.

"This is for your fat earlobe."

She stared at the earring and then at Logan. For the first time, she actually liked him. "There's only one earring."

"This one is from me, and you'll probably get the other one when you see Daniel next. He was going to come with me, but it's crazy at the studio today. He said he'd meet up with you later."

She took the earring out of the box, removed one of her Christmas tree earrings and inserted the new one. She rose on tiptoe and kissed Logan on the cheek. "Thank you."

He grinned. "You're welcome." A faint blush crept up his cheeks.

After he left, she fingered the earring, wondering when Daniel intended to call. Thirty seconds later, he did.

"How about lunch?" Daniel asked. He sounded excited.

"Sorry, I can't today. Every year the past Rose Queens get together for a luncheon, and today is the day." Greer looked forward to it every year. She would pick up Mrs. Allenworth, and the two of them would drive together.

"Sounds like fun. What do you all talk about?"

"We catch up. Who's had babies, who's doing what. The usual girl talk. And we all get dressed up, and we have a purse competition."

"That's a new one. I've heard of shoe competitions, but not purse competitions."

"We give out prizes for the most unique purse, the prettiest, the ugliest, the most different, the cutest, and whatever else we think up."

"I'd like to be a fly on the wall for this event. What kind of purse will you take?"

Greer simply laughed. "I went all out this year and bought the Charlotte Olympia pink poodle purse. I should at least win for cuteness."

"You take this seriously, don't you?"

"Last year I was hurt because my coffin purse didn't win."

"Too macabre, probably."

"I thought for sure I'd win. I even made over my

old Barbie doll into a vampire with fangs and tucked it inside. But I lost the unique purse category to a piñata."

"I think I get it."

"That's because you're competing with your best friend over a float."

Daniel laughed. "How about dinner? And bring the poodle."

"You're on."

The luncheon was held in the permanent head-quarters for the Tournament of Roses Association. Built in 1914 by the chewing gum magnate, William Wrigley Jr., the house was situated on what had once been called Millionaire's Row. Greer loved every inch of the old house, from the high ceilings to the elaborate fireplaces.

All former queens were invited to meet the current queen and her court. The meeting room was decorated with fresh-cut roses at the center of each round table.

"I'm the oldest one left," Mrs. Allenworth said as Greer helped her into the mansion.

"And you can still out-queen any one of us any day of the year."

Though growing stooped, Mrs. Allenworth was still regal, with her snow-white hair pulled into a tasteful French roll at the back of her head. These days, she'd taken to using a cane, but she kept herself in shape by swimming in her indoor pool. She took great pride in the laps she did daily.

"Will you look at that woman," Mrs. Allenworth said, jutting her chin at Zelda Winthrop. "She's still holding court like she is the current queen even though she's on husband number five."

"You're such a gossip."

"We don't want anyone talking about your fat earlobes." Mrs. Allenworth had lived in Pasadena her whole life with her oil magnate husband, who'd only recently retired at the age of eighty-three. She knew everything there was to know about Pasadena society, including where the bodies were buried.

Greer's face scrunched. "You saw that tabloid, did you?"

Before Mrs. Allenworth could reply, Zelda let out a cry. "And look who's here. The woman whose earlobes are up for critical appraisal by the uncouth masses."

Greer groaned.

Zelda drifted toward Greer and Mrs. Allenworth on a cloud of expensive perfume. "In my day, Rose Queens kept their earlobes clean and out of the gossip column."

"Really, my dear," Mrs. Allenworth replied, "has your current husband graduated from high school yet?"

Greer hid a smile. Zelda's husbands grew younger with each marriage.

Zelda waved her hand. "Mrs. Allenworth, you are just so funny. How is that old goat you're married to?"

"He's richer, smarter and more talented than the

last young goat you were married to." Mrs. Allen-worth's voice hinted at laughter.

Zelda's eyes narrowed. She could give and take most anything but amusement at her expense.

"Staying power," Mrs. Allenworth said. "It's all about staying power. Good day, dear. Be off with you. I'm done."

Mrs. Allenworth had won the competition and routed the enemy.

"Thank you for defending me," Greer told her when they were alone. "I was thinking of hitting her with my purse."

"No, dear. That's such a lovely purse, you've got the competition in the bag."

"Is that a pun?"

"You know I'm renowned for my wit." Her eyes twinkled.

Mrs. Allenworth cruised the room, talking with the other queens and the new court. Lunch was perfect, and Greer was completely delighted to win the purse competition, besting Zelda's silly little bag. In true form, Mrs. Allenworth clutched her vintage Chanel, thinking herself above such competitions.

Chapter 8

Daniel walked up Greer's driveway, patting his pocket that contained the hoop earring. He'd come up with the plan as a way to apologize for involving her in the tabloid nonsense, and Logan had thought the idea perfect.

He rang the doorbell. A dog barked inside and the front door swung open, Greer standing back to let him in. It wasn't her beautiful, curve-hugging black dress that drew his attention. It was her earring. In one ear, the twin to Daniel's earring twinkled.

He handed her the box. "Here, so that you're not unbalanced."

"Thank you." She opened the box and drew out the other earring. "You and Logan are certainly inventive." She hooked the hoop through her ear, then handed Daniel her smartphone. "Take a photo of my earrings."

He did and handed her phone back. She grinned as she posted the photo to her Facebook account with the caption, "Fat earlobes slimmed down with diamond earrings. Thank you, Daniel and Logan. They are perfect."

Daniel laughed, happy she was such a good sport.

"How was the luncheon?" he asked as he helped her on with her coat.

"Usually I just walk in under the radar, but today I was the tabloid darling of all the gossips."

"Are you okay with that?" Daniel walked her down the path to his Mercedes.

"I tried not to let it bother me, but a couple of the girls today were particularly nasty. Especially after I won the purse competition." She held up her pink poodle purse.

"Good for you." He opened the car door, and she slid in.

"Where are we off to eat?"

"Georgio's. Have you ever eaten there?"

"That's across the street from Vroman's Bookstore."

"That's the place. My parents recommended it. And they don't recommend restaurants very often. Then maybe a late stroll into Vroman's. It's my favorite bookstore in the whole world."

"Mine, too."

The drive to the restaurant took ten minutes. A valet took his Mercedes, and they entered the romantically lit restaurant and were seated at a booth with a high back that went to the ceiling, giving them unusual privacy.

After a discreet waitress took their drink order and left them to read the menu, Daniel dug his phone out of his pocket.

"I want to show you something." He scrolled down and then handed her the phone. "Read those comments."

"I hope they aren't about another of my body parts."

"Just read," he ordered.

She read. A dozen comments under his weekly blog, which was about the Rose Parade, ran from nasty to admiring. "Some people seem to think the Rose Parade is frivolous," she said.

"And would you respond?"

He loved the way her face took on a serious look as she contemplated her answer. "We need things that are beautiful. We need pageantry. Yes, the world's got problems, but we need things to remind us that there are good things about the human race. I think the Rose Parade does that. Detractors of any event are going to come out of the woodwork to complain about whatever. I need to be above that. And let's talk about the millions of dollars poured into the Pasadena economy by the people who come to view the parade. That money keeps jobs here.

"And the parade sheds lights on some social issues, too. After I designed the Humane Society float, local shelters were practically cleaned out of adoptable animals. I think the parade does a lot of positive work, and anyone who says otherwise is just mean. Yeah, the parade is a lot more commercial now than it was in the past, but it still does a lot of good things."

He smiled broadly. "That's exactly what I want for tomorrow's segment. I want your passion, your fire, your love for the parade."

She eyed him skeptically. "Was this a test?"

"What's the right answer to that? I mean an answer that will get me into your bed tonight."

She grinned at him. "Silence."

"Did I tell you that your pink poodle purse is absolutely great?"

She reached across the table and took his hand. "You did, and for that you get another night in my bed."

Greer walked ahead of him and unlocked her front door. "Don't dawdle."

"What's the hurry?"

She tossed her purse on the couch and slid out of her shoes. "I have needs."

Well, so did he, he thought as he pulled off his shirt and tossed it on the floor. "I do need fulfillment."

"Good."

He watched her dress fly over her shoulder and nearly hit him in the face. By the time he got to her bedroom, she was standing naked by the bed. He walked over to her, and she reached out and put her hand on his chest. He grabbed her wandering hand and in an instant had her flat on her back. He bent over until he rested between her thighs, his chest crushing hers.

Greer wrapped her legs around his hips and arched her back. "This is going to be so much fun."

"I will do my best." He lowered his head and took a nipple in his mouth, sucking the bud into a peak.

A fractured moan broke from her lips. He nipped her skin, and Greer trembled. Daniel laughed. She squirmed, their skin sliding together, fanning the raging inferno inside him. He needed her so badly. He grabbed her wrists together and held them in one hand over her head. Slowly he trailed his fingers over her breasts to her waist. Heat burned his fingertips, and his heart raced as he watched the muscles in her stomach contract at his touch.

"Make love to me," she whispered.

He licked the underside of her breast.

Greer raised her legs higher on his hips. She struggled to free her wrists. "I want to touch you."

Daniel rose and pulled her up, chest to chest. He took her mouth in a hard kiss meant to mark her as his. His lips did the job, and when the kiss ended, he was consumed by a need he could not ignore.

All his control had waltzed right out the door when she'd begged him to make love to her. Daniel didn't know what demon possessed him, but he wanted to consume all of her. One taste of her was worth anything. He cupped her breasts, and when he teased her nipples, she wriggled her body against him.

His pulse raced. He was ready to take her hard. "You want it?"

"Now!" she insisted.

He turned her around and balanced on his knees behind her. Gripping her hips, he pulled her backside to him and plunged into her, burying himself deep inside her tight flesh. He held her hips against him with one hand, digging his fingers in her soft skin, and he used his other hand to tease her clitoris. Each stroke sent a deep shudder through her. Her breathing was harsh as he thrust inside her. Her internal muscles tightened around him, and he could feel the sweat beading on his brow. He squeezed his eyes shut, focusing on the feel of her sleek skin against his. He didn't have much control left, he was so overloaded by the sensation.

He felt her contract against him as an orgasm ripped through her. His thrusts turned hard and demanding. Sensations tore through him, sensations he'd never felt when making love to a woman before her. He clenched his jaw, feeling all his muscles tense as he pounded into her willing body.

His own orgasm neared, and he thrust harder, his brain clouding with thoughts of her.

He rocked against her. Her back went rigid and stiff as she gripped the bed covers in her fists.

His heart beat like a jackhammer, as if it would burst from his chest. The blood in his veins roared with passion. He withdrew almost entirely out of her and gave one last heaving stroke. His orgasm exploded, and he spilled everything he had inside her. A guttural cry left his mouth, and he began to shake.

Greer went down to the bed, turning as she lay

back, and pulled him into her arms. She caught her breath and snuggled up to him, her skin slick with perspiration. The musky scent of unbridled sex hung in the room. Daniel pushed a strand of hair off her flushed cheek. His hand lingered on her soft skin as he tried to form the words to tell her how he felt, but anything he thought to say seemed inadequate.

She smiled at him, her breasts rising with each breath. "Wow! That was so…naughty."

What they had just done was way beyond naughty. He propped himself on his elbow. "Priceless."

She giggled and rolled on top of him, giving him a quick kiss.

He grinned.

"Good." She kissed his chest.

If he was honest with himself, he didn't want to let her go just yet.

The next day, Greer arrived at the studio and had to traverse a gauntlet of paparazzi and overeager fans. Cameras flashed in front of her eyes, and a barrage of questions was shouted at her. Someone pushed a mic in her face and it bumped against her nose. She stopped and glared at the reporter, who stepped back, looking chagrinned. She shielded her face as she pushed through to the door. She didn't know how Logan and Daniel could ignore the constant bombardment of inane questions. Who cared if she wore her shoes to bed or not? And it was nobody's business what brand of underwear she wore.

Daniel had told her to ignore them, give them nothing. But from the number of flashes in her eyes, she figured her photo would still be gracing the cover of *Celebrity Buzz*.

After a quick makeup session, she took her seat on the set across from Daniel. Despite several appearances, the camera eye staring at her still made her uncomfortable. No matter how carefully she dressed to bolster her confidence, she knew she was under a microscope and felt awkward.

He reached out and squeezed her hand, letting her know he had her back, and she felt better instantly.

Because of the time constraint of television, he got right to the point. "You ready to do a little history of the Rose Parade and Isabella Coleman?"

Greer nodded. She was delighted to give that information once the camera was rolling. "The first Rose Parade was in 1890 and consisted of horse-drawn buggies decorated with ribbons and flowers from Pasadena gardens," she explained. She had brought photos of the early carriages, and now she saw them on the monitor facing her and Daniel. "The idea was to promote the beauty of the West by holding a series of games such as chariot races, jousting tournaments and polo. The events were preceded by the parade, which ran down Colorado Boulevard."

"And to think, that small parade has evolved into something so elaborate today," Daniel said, a touch of wonder in his voice.

"We have the parade as we know it today thanks to Isabella Coleman. She was a native of Pasadena and a pioneer in float design. She was still in her teens when she designed and built her own float. By the time she was nineteen, she was designing floats for clients. She was quite the entrepreneur."

A photo of Isabella as a young woman appeared on the monitor, surrounded by trophies and ribbons. Greer loved this photo because it showed what one determined woman could do in the face of so many challenges.

"She completely transformed the float design process," Greer continued, "and was the first to glue flower petals onto the designs and put flowers in little glass vials filled with water to keep them fresh. She designed the first steel undercarriages, and by the time she was thirty, she'd won numerous trophies and awards. She also pioneered the participation of women in the parade planning."

Greer owed Isabella a lot. The woman had done more than just pave the way for females. She'd set the foundations of the parade.

"Isabella Coleman sounds pretty impressive," Daniel said.

"She was," Greer said with enthusiasm. "She never considered herself a businesswoman, but her design business kept her family afloat when her husband lost his job during the Great Depression."

"In that time, women weren't allowed to be business-oriented," Daniel said.

"Thank goodness times have changed. I probably wouldn't be able to do what I do if not for her, and there were times when it wasn't easy. When the first African American Rose Queen was nominated, I wasn't even born, and my dad used to say that people complained about Pasadena going to hell in a hand-basket. In 1958 a queen was disqualified because she was biracial. And now we've had a Hispanic, an Asian and an African American queen as a matter of course, and no one blinks an eye." She went on to talk about Los Angeles being one of the most diverse cities in the United States, and she liked to think the diversity was represented by the Rose Queen and her court.

Daniel smiled and nodded his head. He understood the importance of diversity.

"My grandfather," she continued, "was an actor in the forties and fifties and did pretty well for himself. He bought a house in Pasadena, and since then my family has been entrenched in the culture that is Pasadena."

Daniel made a few comments, then wrapped up the segment. "We'll now pause for this commercial break. And when we return, we'll have Heather Applegate on weather, Christine Matthews with traffic and Wilma Alvarez with the news."

The director held up a hand. When he counted down to one, Daniel stood, removed his mic and held out a hand to Greer. "Once again, nicely done, Greer." Despite his professional demeanor, his eyes seemed to bore through her when he looked at her so intensely. Their brown depths told her more than the simple compliment. Much more.

She wanted him just as badly. She wanted to step into his arms and kiss him right there, but she was aware of all the eyes staring at them on the set.

Instead, she let him escort her back to his office, keeping her hands at her sides and away from the temptation that was Daniel.

Once his office door was closed behind them, he turned and kissed her. His kiss thrilled her right down to her toes.

When he had his fill of her, he pulled back and studied her. "What are you doing for Christmas Eve?"

It took her a moment and a few breaths to calm her racing pulse. When she was finally able to speak, she replied, "Traditionally, my family doesn't gather on Christmas Eve. We get together Christmas morning, have breakfast, open our gifts and have an early dinner, eating ourselves into oblivion."

He laughed. "Sounds like my family. We have our own tradition. On Christmas Eve, we go to a performance of *The Nutcracker*. I have an extra ticket. Would you like to be my date?"

Greer hadn't seen *The Nutcracker* in years, and she was thrilled Daniel asked. "Yes. I don't have any other plans, other than maybe finishing my decorations. We rotate houses for Christmas, and this year it's my turn."

"I can help with that." Daniel gave her a hopeful look.

She laughed. "And I'll take it. Because starting the day after Christmas, I won't be sleeping until the parade."

"My last segment will be from the staging area."

"What will you do if neither one of you wins the Sweepstakes Trophy?"

Daniel looked thoughtful. "Logan and I are so used to one of us coming away a winner that I hadn't considered it."

"There are going to be seventy floats vying for the different trophies. It's not just you and Logan."

"I'll talk to Logan and see what he says. Maybe we just have to win a trophy in any category. If push comes to shove, we'll flip a coin."

"You'd best have that backup plan implemented just to be safe. There are too many variables to assure you'll win something. It's just doesn't work that way."

He kissed the end of her nose. "I'll keep that in mind when I talk to Logan."

"Okay, then. I need to get going." She grabbed her purse and turned for the door. But Daniel reached her and pulled her around into his arms.

"Don't leave without this." Then he kissed her.

She left the studio and walked through the gauntlet of paparazzi shouting questions at her. Who did she like better—Logan or Daniel? How would she rate their prowess in bed? By the time she shoved through to her car and eased out of the parking structure, she was trembling. But she didn't know whether it was from the cameras that had been shoved in her face or Daniel's kiss.

Chapter 9

Greer loved the lot her house sat on. Shaped like an L with the house on the bottom, the property afforded her a huge garden going up from the left side. On the other side she'd placed a gazebo so she could sit and look out over the ravine that bordered her lot and watch the wildlife—mostly deer, raccoons and possums.

Her favorite part of the interior was the large fireplace in her living room. There was something so special, so cozy about sitting there watching the fire on a cool evening. But it was only late morning and she already had the fire going. It seemed the perfect touch to Christmas Eve morning, the perfect way to get her in the mood for holiday decorating. She'd gotten the boxes of decorations out of the garage, and in one corner of her living room she'd placed a live Christmas tree. After Christmas, she would find a place in the yard to plant it. She already had three trees along the left property line to mark the three years she'd lived in the house.

She was about to unwrap the tree ornaments when Daniel pulled into her driveway. She went to the front door to greet him. Cold air swirled in with him. A fine drizzle had started, and little droplets clung to his hair.

He held up a takeout bag. "I brought lunch as ordered."

She grinned and kissed him. "Thank you." She led the way down the hall to the kitchen, where she grabbed dishes and set them on trays to carry into the living room after they made their plates.

"I like your Christmas shirt and hat."

"Thank you." Her mother had given her the classic red sweatshirt with Santa in his sleigh with little puffs of cotton for his hat and suit. The hat was her own addition, a traditional stocking with Merry Christmas embroidered on the white band.

In the living room, she pulled two wing chairs up to the fire, and they chatted about holiday traditions as they ate.

"The day after Thanksgiving," Daniel said, "my brothers and sisters and I head over to our parents' house, and we set up the outside lights and decorations. Every house on the block is decorated for Christmas, except for one."

"Who's the Scrooge?"

"It rotates. We have this huge sign that says Scrooge Lives Here, and whoever is Scrooge for the year gets it."

"On my street, only a few houses decorate," Greer said as she munched on her ham sandwich. "But my family tradition is that we all have homemade ornaments. I started making them when I was seven, and since then I've made hundreds to decorate all our trees."

"I'm anxious to see them."

"Pull that box over." She pointed at a brown box with Christmas Ornaments neatly stenciled on the side.

She slid down to sit on the floor and pulled the lid off. Inside, each ornament was carefully wrapped in tissue paper and nestled in its own compartment. She unwrapped a clear glass ball with Santa painted on it. She handed it to Daniel. "Every ornament has a story," she explained. "I painted that one when I was ten. My mother didn't want mass-produced ornaments. She wanted unique and personal. She loves a good story."

She unwrapped another glass ornament with crutches painted on them. "This is to commemorate Rachel breaking her leg when she fell off a float." Rachel had been in her freshman year at UCLA, Greer recalled, and trying to get around campus on crutches had been a huge challenge. Her parents had finally rented a golf cart for her.

Daniel sat on the floor across from her, his lunch forgotten as he opened a box containing a miniature

Christmas village. "Wow. Did you paint these?" He pulled out a ceramic building with surf boards leaning against the side. And a bakery with nothing but cookies showing in the tiny windows.

She nodded. "The buildings go on the mantel."

He pulled out a figure dressed in shorts and a brightly colored Hawaiian shirt.

"Surfer Santa," Greer said with a grin. "I didn't want a traditional village with snow. I wanted a California Christmas with lots of color and things that are unique to California."

He pulled out the Hollywood sign with a sleigh and reindeer balanced on the top and the lead reindeer wearing a Santa hat. She'd made four of them and given them to her family. "My mother would love something like this," he said.

"Give her that one," Greer said.

"But…"

"I insist." She leaned back against the chair and watched him as he pulled several more ceramic buildings and houses out of the box. "I'm surprised you wanted to help me. Not many men I know are interested in decorating for Christmas."

He sat back and smiled at her. "When I was a kid, my parents were on the road a lot. Christmas was the one holiday of the year that they were guaranteed to be home no matter what type of gig was offered them. They turned down some pretty heavy offers just to be home at Christmas. They wanted the time to be special. Dad would cook up a storm, and our house would smell so delicious that I would invite all my friends over just to experience the wonderful scents. Mom would take each one of us shopping, and we got to spend the whole day just with her.

"My happiest memories are of when it was my turn to go shopping with her, we went to Macy's and she let me give my list to Santa. We shopped, went to lunch and discussed getting a special gift for my sister because that year I'd drawn her name in our little lottery. I wanted to get a Barbie doll for Lola. She was maybe five or six. I was eight. I don't ever remember her playing with dolls, but in my head, I thought if she had one, she'd play with it. Mom knew Lola better than I and somehow managed to steer me toward an electric keyboard. And to this day, Lola loves that keyboard. She still composes on it and told me she thinks about me every time she puts her fingers on the keys." His face lit up with the beauty of that memory.

Greer's heart did a little lurch. Daniel Torres had made his way into her life, and she liked having him in it. In fact, she loved being with him. He was more than just her lover. He'd become her friend, and they shared the kind of friendship that would last a life-time.

"My favorite gift," Greer said, "was when Santa, aka my parents, gave me an artist's set of paints, colored pencils, chalk and brushes. It came in a beautiful wood box with a thick pad of drawing paper and an easel. I still have the box, even though it's beat up and cracking. I think it's pretty amazing that parents know us better than we know ourselves."

That's the kind of parent Greer wanted to be, and

in her fantasy, Daniel replaced the faceless, name-less man who had always been there with her. She pulled her knees up to her chest and wrapped her arms around them. The thought that she wanted Daniel to stay in her life startled her. She wished she could take time to explore the idea, but her house needed decorating.

Daniel seemed in no hurry, still looking through her ornaments. "We're lucky, you know. Logan's parents had the money to give him everything and ended up giving him a credit card and setting him loose to shop for himself." He smiled as a memory must have hit him. "One year he brought the card to my mom, who got permission to use it, went shopping and wrapped up a couple of gifts for him and put them under our tree. He told me that was his best Christmas ever." He held up another ornament with a portrait painted on it. "Who's this?"

"My grandmother, DeeDee Courtland," Greer said. "She's gone now, but I wanted her to be a part of Christmas forever. She lived with us when I was young, and she was a major influence in our lives. She took care of my sisters and me while our parents were getting the company off the ground." Greer still missed her even though she'd passed on six years ago. Nostalgia overwhelmed her, and she felt tears gather at the corners of her eyes. She brushed them away impatiently and stood up to start decorating.

By the time they were ready to leave for the theater, her house was completely decorated. The tree was laden with dozens of ornaments, twinkling lights and a silver garland. Her cheerful Christmas village had been arranged on the fireplace mantel, and lights framed the windows of each room facing the street. She'd hung Christmas towels in the bathrooms and tied large ribbons around them. Last, she'd attached a wreath on the front door, and Daniel had hung mistletoe from the arched entry into her living room.

After they dressed in their formal clothes, Daniel grabbed her and kissed her deeply under the mistletoe.

"I love this tradition," he said, his lips warm on hers, his hand tight against her back.

Every part of her body tingled with a growing passion that filled her.

"Thank you for all your help and for sharing your memories," she said when he released her.

"I enjoyed today. I enjoy being with you. A lot." He caressed her chin with one finger, slowly moving it down her throat to her cleavage. "When the parade is finally over, I want to spend more time with you. I have vacation time coming. Let's go do something different."

"What do you mean by different?" she asked as he draped her heavy cashmere shawl over her shoulders to ward off the night chill.

"Let's go see some snow. My parents have a cabin at Lake Tahoe. I hear the skiing is pretty good this year."

She thought about it. She had to be in Rio de Janeiro at the end of January to work on the Mardi Gras float her parents had been commissioned to build. "I

have a counteroffer. How about Rio instead? I have
to be there for the final prep work on a float, but I
could take an extra week, and we'll do Mardi Gras
Brazilian style."

He thought for a moment. "I'm in. I've never been
to Rio. Mardi Gras sounds like fun."

"I do have to work, but it's not as intense as the
Rose Parade." Besides, she had a crew in Rio; her
being there was more a formality to show her family's support.

"Then Rio it is."

She felt absurdly pleased, and happiness filled her
as she walked out to his car.

The days after Christmas were pure chaos. Floats
were jammed into the huge tent in long rows. Volunteers mobbed the flower tent, getting what they
needed from the areas secured for their floats, then
swarmed over the floats like an army of worker ants.
Each float might need ten thousand or more pounds
of flowers, flower petals, seeds and organic matter.
Loud laughter, chatter from the volunteers and the
sound of hammers added to the confusion. The overpowering scent of flowers filled the air. From now
until the night before of the parade, flowers would
be delivered nonstop.

Diagrams of the flower arrangement hung on a
bulletin board filled with clipboards. Each clipboard
had a senior volunteer's name who would then direct
other workers. Chelsea oversaw quality control for
all the floats, while Greer managed the senior volun-

teers. Rachel was in charge of the flower inventory. The three sisters had it down to a science, organizing the thousands of man-hours that went into the final preparation in round-the-clock shifts.

Greer parked her parents' Winnebago at the edge of the parking lot. From now until the end of the parade, she and her sisters would live in it to oversee their little army and be on site for last-minute problems.

Today Daniel's film crew was there doing a few preview segments. Tomorrow he would do his whole show from the tent, interviewing volunteers, talking to the different designers and filming the last minute excitement as the floats changed from welded steel skeletons to completely decorated floral masterpieces.

He stopped at his float and motioned Greer over. She held her clipboard close to her chest. When Rod Ortega, one of the senior volunteers, started her way, she held up a finger, asking him to wait.

"I just wanted you to take a moment to breathe," Daniel told her when she'd walked over to him. "You're running around like a madwoman. By the time the parade happens, you're going to be exhausted. How do you cope?"

"It's like watching your children in a beauty pageant and hoping no one has a wardrobe malfunction."

"What is the parade version of a wardrobe malfunction?" he asked.

"The wing on your butterfly falling off." She didn't add that it already had because she didn't want him worrying needlessly.

"Do things like that happen?"

"All the time."

As if on cue, a crash sounded somewhere in the tent, and every head turned toward it.

"Maybe I should check that out." Daniel glanced at the director, who nodded.

"You do that." Greer turned toward Rod Ortega to hear what his latest problem was. "What's up, Rod?"

"The roses from Venezuela may not make it in time. The plane is having engine trouble, and they won't be off the ground for another twenty-four hours."

Greer wasn't surprised. If a problem was going to happen, this was the week for it to happen. "I'll call Mrs. Allenworth. She'll let us raid her greenhouse. Get a team over there."

Rod nodded and walked away, gesturing at a couple of volunteers to come with him. Greer reached for her phone.

Chelsea approached, looking somewhat concerned. "The Trident float has a crack in the plastic on the skirt."

"Fill it with airplane glue. See, we're fine," Greer said.

Chelsea relaxed a bit…until someone dropped a bag of sunflower seeds, and the seeds scattered everywhere.

Even Greer rubbed her temples. A headache was starting, and she didn't have time for one now.

She stopped at the Brocade Industries float to find that one of the volunteers had put the wrong flower on the playground designed to hold children on swings and on the glider. Since the orchids, enclosed in glass vials of water, were simply pushed through the chicken wire, the fix was easy. She smiled pleasantly at the volunteer, explained where the orchids went and allowed him to figure out the rest.

She turned and found Logan Pierce standing behind her. "What are you doing here?"

"Want to sneak out and leave all this madness behind?"

She shook her head, grinning. "Will you stop."

He patted her arm. "Since we might end up being family…"

"What do you mean by that?"

He shrugged. "Daniel is madly in love with you."

She gave his statement some thought. "Will you just stop flirting with me?"

"I am going to have to stop, but I don't want to. I like that Daniel gets his back up when I flirt. I don't get much over on him."

Greer closed her eyes as she spied another volunteer approaching, no doubt with another question or crisis. When she opened them, she turned to Logan. "Much as I'd like to take a break, if I step outside, there will be a score of paparazzi waiting to take pictures of me and exploit our alleged love triangle. I don't have time for that."

"I can protect you."

"Go away, Logan." She pushed him away and turned to the volunteer patiently waiting for her.

* * *

That night in the Winnebago, Greer sat with her feet up on the coffee table, trying not to fall asleep. Chelsea had made sandwiches before heading back for the evening shift, but Greer was too tired to eat. The door to the RV slammed open and Rachel stepped inside. She handed Greer a tabloid.

"You need to see this," Rachel said, sitting down in the chair opposite Greer.

"I can't."

Rachel held up the tabloid. Her house was shown prominently on the front page. "Logan Pierce, Daniel Torres and Greer Courtland's Secret Love Nest." Greer covered her eyes. Would these infuriating stories never end?

"Burn it," Greer said.

"You're taking all the fun out of it," Rachel said.

"I hope they didn't print my address."

"You're in luck there. No address and no location of any kind. Their legal department probably won't let them. Printing your address could be construed as harassment and leave them open to a huge lawsuit."

"I don't get it. I'm nobody."

"You may be a regular woman, but you're a regular woman dating a celebrity. They keep harping on the Rose Queen angle because it's glamorous and sexy."

"It was a job," Greer said with a tired sigh. "I didn't have to wear a swimsuit or play some musical instrument like a kazoo or answer the question of how I would save the world, or the whales. Or tell the world I'm not just a pretty face because I read Freud or Kierkegaard."

Rachel just laughed. "You're taking this way too seriously."

"They're not looking through your trash can."

"They're looking through your trash can?"

She nodded. "And they don't have the courtesy of even putting the trash back. Mrs. Kelly across the street has been giving me the evil eye all month as though I desecrated the neighborhood."

"Wow," Rachel said. "Is there anything worthwhile in your trash?"

"Not anymore. Once I figured out what they were doing, I started bringing my trash to the office." She discarded it in the huge Dumpsters that were kept under lock and key at the rear of the building. "I had no idea I created that much trash in the course of a week."

"Carbon footprints say a lot about you, sis."

A knock sounded at the door, and Greer hauled herself to her aching feet to open it. Rod Ortega grinned at her. "We need you in the tent."

Greer sighed. "I'm coming." She grabbed the sandwich Chelsea had left for her on the counter and ate it as she stepped out, ready to take on the next problem.

Daniel wandered through the tent, trailed by his cameraman, soundman and director and all their assistants. As he walked, he interviewed one of the float judges.

"What do you look at when you're judging a float,

Mrs. Barret?" Daniel asked the trim, petite woman standing next to him.

Mrs. Barret smiled graciously at him. "We have a list of items that we grade on, including theme, application, decorations, overall color scheme, beauty and subject matter. The day before the parade, every float must be in parade-ready condition with all the riders on board and in their places for the final judging."

"The judging must take all day."

"And sometimes more."

"Thank you, Mrs. Barret."

She nodded and walked on, her expert eyes already judging another float on her list.

His next interview was set up in front of his float. He motioned over the senior volunteer who'd introduced himself earlier as Rod Ortega.

"How long have you been a volunteer, Mr. Ortega?" he asked politely. In the last six weeks, he'd learned so much about float construction that sometimes the knowledge invaded his dreams.

"Thirty-five years," Rod Ortega said. "Started when I was eleven. My parents had just moved to Sierra Madre and somehow got involved with the Sierra Madre float association. I met my wife there, and now she and the kids all volunteer, too. My youngest is six, and she's already thinking about a career as a float designer."

"Must be hectic." Daniel said, admiring the man's determination.

"It's all the last-minute, unforeseen things that get to you. But I have a system, and Greer is a delight to work with. She never loses her cool no matter what catastrophe happens. Despite everything, this is fun."

Daniel thought Greer was a delight to work with, too. Even though he hadn't seen her since their evening at *The Nutcracker*, they talked every other day, though last night's conversation had ended on a petite snore from her end of the phone. He missed being with her. She had grown on him in a way no other woman had. He hated not seeing her, not being with her. A tiny ache of loneliness disappeared when she appeared at the edge of his vision and walked down the aisle, her clipboard in hand. She looked beat. He wanted to soothe the tired lines across her forehead.

"What do you get out of all this?" he asked Rod Ortega as he forced his attention back to the interview.

"Other than ringside seats, I feel I bring a little bit of happiness to the world. I love that my kids' faces just shine when they see the float they worked on all finished and ready for the parade route. Plus, I get to do something with my children that I hope will provide them with happy memories all their lives. I know I have a lot of happy memories of being here with my parents."

"I suppose your parents have retired and passed on the legacy to you."

"Not a chance," Rod said with a smile. He pointed at a tiny woman clinging to a scaffold as she painted what looked like glue on the wing of a bird. Then she poured black seeds on the area. Some clung and others fell. "That's my mom over there. I don't think she's going to stop doing this. She loves it. And my dad is over at the flower tent. He supervises the flower inventory with Rachel Courtland."

Daniel turned to face the camera. "There you have it, folks. The rose parade is a family legacy passed down from generation to generation. And now for a commercial break. We'll be back for the final segment of our show today at the Rose Parade staging tent in just a few minutes."

The director called, "Clear." Daniel shook hands with Rod Ortega then decided he needed to be with Greer for a few minutes before he had to return in front of the camera and walked over.

Greer tilted her head up to him, and he kissed her. "It's crazy in here."

"This is the best time. My favorite part."

As he looked closer, he saw she did appear exhilarated. Her face was slightly flushed, her eyes bright and excited despite the dark circles ringing them. A flower petal clung to her T-shirt, and a couple of narrow green leaves were caught in her hair. The aroma of flowers had been overpowering at first, but Daniel had finally grown used to it.

"When does the judging start?" He was anxious to get to that part of the parade.

"Preliminaries are tomorrow. The final judging the day after." A volunteer approached her and asked a question about a particular flower she couldn't find, and Greer told her to check in the flower tent.

Daniel slid an arm around her waist and pulled her close. "How about a quick dinner later?"

"A quick dinner is going to be fifteen minutes, twenty max," she said with a harried look on her face.

"I'll bring the food."

"Bring enough for Rachel and Chelsea, too. Lots of protein. We need energy. Tonight is going to be an all-nighter for us."

Rod Ortega grabbed Greer's arm. "I need you. Sorry, Mr. Torres." He dragged Greer away.

She gave a half turn and waved at Daniel. He waved back, realizing that this woman had turned into the love of his life. Falling in love had been so gradual, he hadn't realized it until this moment. She was feisty, independent, practical and perfect. So perfect he wanted to rush right over to her and tell her, even as he watched her climb aboard a float to study whatever Rod was pointing at.

The women he'd dated before Greer had been so different from her. The starlets, the ingenues, the models had never shown the level of independence Greer had. She made her own decisions and stuck by them. She didn't expect him to choose what she should eat, or wear, or even think. Daniel had almost fallen into the same trap as those models. He hadn't wanted to be bothered with small decisions, with the little things in his life, until he realized other people were making bigger and bigger decisions on his behalf and he put a stop to it. Greer never expected anyone else to make decisions for her.

Daniel watched her. She knelt down on the float while talking to Rod, who nodded. Then she stood, smiled at Rod and patted his shoulder. Daniel could almost imagine her soothing him over something. Then she jumped down from the float, summoned by Chelsea further down the aisle.

The director tapped Daniel on the shoulder. Daniel hurried back to his temporary set, ready to film the final segment of the show.

Chapter 10

Daniel was nervous. He stood in his spot on the finished float. Nick and Michelle on their dance floor performed a simple waltz to the music they'd chosen. The fourth person on his float was Cecile Holloway. He had chosen her for her ability to transcend the barriers forced on women actors. To him, she had finally come into her own, still a butterfly at eighty-three.

Cecile was an Oscar contender for her last role. She fumbled with the buckle on her safety belt, and Daniel reached over to help her.

"Thank you, Daniel." Her tone was as gracious as always. "I've always wanted to be in the Rose Parade. This is a dream come true. I tried out for Rose Queen when I was in high school but wasn't chosen."

Daniel grinned at her. "I'm glad I could make your

dream come true. This is a celebration of life, and you epitomize exactly that. You're still in high demand in an industry where most actresses are on the shelf by the time they're forty. I wanted to show the world that a person's value isn't about how they look, but how they think."

"I'm eighty-three years old, and sometimes my thought processes stutter."

"But they seem to stutter in the right direction and are still firing on all cylinders. Even I have senior moments, and I'm only thirty."

Cecile laughed. The sound of the hydraulics was a constant buzz as the butterfly wings rose and fell.

Daniel watched the judges as they walked around the float, making notes on their clipboards. He couldn't contain his nerves.

Down the aisle he could just see Logan's float, specifically the huge rainbow that went from front to back. The float was so beautiful, it took Daniel's breath away. In fact, all the floats were gorgeous, and he wondered how the judges could decide who won which trophy.

Greer walked down the aisle with Chelsea. She stopped to give an encouraging smile at Daniel.

Finally the judges ended their scrutiny and walked away. Daniel's breath exploded out so forcefully, he realized he'd been holding it in.

He unbuckled his safety belt and then helped Cecile down a set of stairs on the side of the float.

"What do you think?" he asked Greer.

"I think you have a good shot, but then again, I

think all my babies are beautiful." She grinned at him, her face flushed. "So now we're going to check and make sure the float engine is working properly." She spoke into the walkie-talkie she held in one hand. "Start her up, Rod."

"Roger that," Rod responded.

Nick and Michelle joined Daniel and Greer, all waiting anxiously. The engine sounded rough, as though it were coughing. Then a cloud of white smoke billowed upward.

"Greer," Rod said, his voice crackling over her headset. "We have problem."

Greer said, "We have less than twenty-four hours to fix it."

Daniel shrugged off his jacket. He climbed up the stairs and hauled open the lid over the driver's compartment. "My turn to take a look." He held out a hand for Rod, who climbed out.

"I'll get my tools," Rod said. "This isn't a catastrophe." Then he added solemnly, "I hope."

Daniel didn't answer. He unbuttoned the cuffs on his shirt and rolled up the sleeves.

Daniel was darn sexy with his sleeves turned up as he slid under the chassis on the wheeled platform to take a look at the motor. He rolled back out, a smear of grease on his face.

"What's wrong with the motor?" Greer asked.

"Sounds like a blown gasket," Daniel replied. "I'm going to need some parts. I'll make a list, and you can send someone to the nearest auto parts store and get what I need."

"How long will it take?" Greer was always ready for the unexpected to happen, but a blown gasket didn't sound like a good thing.

"I need to get at the engine. We may need to pull it out."

"What about a new engine?"

"Do you know how much these things weigh?" Daniel asked. "I can fix it."

"And I'll help," Rod said as he dropped his toolbox on the ground.

Greer worked hard to keep her nerves under control. Catastrophes happened, but this was the first one to occur within twenty-four hours of parade day. "You can fix motors?"

"Yes. Along with collecting cars, I also work on them. Besides, with a lot of siblings, there wasn't always extra money, so I had to learn to do all sorts of things as a kid. If I wanted a car, I learned how to take care of it."

"Wow," Greer said, admiration filling her. Another part of Daniel had just been revealed. He could not only explain the mysteries of the stars to her but also fix a motor. He'd be handy to have around the next time she had a flat tire and didn't want to get her hands dirty.

"When are the winners announced for the trophies?" he asked as he rapidly wrote his list. He leaned against the float, a frown on his face.

"They're not announced. You'll see." She patted his arm. "Stop worrying and fix the motor."

He saluted her. "Will do." He and Rod opened the canopy over the motor and spent a few minutes looking it over.

Greer turned away, ready to tackle the other minor issues that had arisen. She had a feeling this was going to be the longest day of her life.

Greer stifled a yawn. The Winnebago was chilly, the heat just turning on. The night was so cold, Greer could see her breath as she opened the refrigerator to grab something to eat. She finally found some sandwich meat and two slices of bread.

Rachel was repairing the area of the float around the engine canopy that had been damaged by Daniel and Rod as they worked, and Chelsea was at a last-minute meeting with the float committee.

A knock sounded on the door. Greer opened it and found Daniel standing outside, a garment bag flung over one shoulder. Grease stained his hands. Lines of fatigue scored his forehead.

"Can I spend the night?" he asked. "I'm too tired to drive home. And I have to be back at two a.m." Daniel gave her a hopeful look.

"You're more than welcome to sleep here."

"Aren't your sisters spending the night, too?"

"You can join the slumber party. I see you're already prepared." She nodded toward the garment bag.

He stepped into the Winnebago. "I picked my suit

up at the cleaners this morning before I came over for the rehearsal."

She stepped back. "Are you hungry?"

"I could eat."

She opened a cabinet and pulled out a bag of cheese doodles.

He looked at the bag and then at her.

"This is how we celebrate New Year's Eve. Cheese doodles and braiding our hair."

He dropped the garment bag over a chair, and with one eyebrow raised, he broke open the bag. "I'll take the cheese doodles, but my hair is way too short to braid."

She laughed. "Sit down. I can make you a sandwich." She opened the refrigerator for two more slices of bread. After liberally spreading mayo and adding turkey meat, lettuce and cheese, she turned to hand the sandwich to Daniel, only to find his head leaning back against the wall, his eyes closed. She set the plate in front of him and sat down across from him to eat her own sandwich. When she finished, she made up a bed for Daniel.

The Winnebago slept eight. Two sets of bunk beds resided on either side of the RV, which was usually where Greer and her sisters slept. The master bedroom at the very back was reserved for her parents. Daniel was too tall for the bunk beds, and since her parents had decided to stay in a local hotel, the master bedroom would work for him.

When she finished, she took a quick shower and then went to wake Daniel, only to find him eating.

"When you're done eating, take a shower. I made up the master bedroom for you."

"Want to share it with me?" he asked with a flirty grin.

"No. I need my rest, and so do you." She glanced at the clock over the sink. "It'll be two a.m. before you know it. Let's get some sleep."

Daniel looked disappointed. He finished his sandwich and dragged himself to the bathroom while Greer crawled into her bunk. Later, Greer heard him fall onto the bed just before Chelsea dragged herself in. Greer had no idea what time Rachel returned, but when her next thought surfaced, her alarm was blasting away. Two in the morning was not a civilized time to wake, yet she had no choice. It was parade day. Despite her fatigue, Greer had bowls of cereal ready by the time everyone else woke.

"Eat some cereal," she told Daniel as she emptied her own bowl, went to the sink and washed it. Rachel emerged from the tiny bathroom yawning while Chelsea tugged a brush through her hair. Four adults made the Winnebago feel crowded.

Daniel sat at the table, looking out the window at the parking lot. Absolute chaos reigned as floats exited the tent and headed down to the parade start. He marveled at how the parade supervisors got the massive floats into position.

"When do I find out that I won?" Daniel asked.

"The winners will know at the beginning of the parade route. Boy Scouts bearing banners will step in front of the float as it moves into its parade position. Did I ask you if you had a plan B in place? What will you do if neither of you wins the Sweepstakes Trophy?"

"Logan and I will talk later. We did consider the possibility. At least, I did, but Logan didn't want to think about it much with his big ego."

Greer laughed. "Ouch."

"Are you sure you two are best friends?" Chelsea asked as she downed a huge mug of coffee.

"That's how boys play."

"You two are grown men," Chelsea said.

"Only on the outside," Daniel said with a chuckle. "What do the trophies look like? I just realized you have all these photos in your office, but no trophies."

"You won't win a physical trophy. You receive a beautifully framed photo with a banner on it announcing which trophy the float won."

"All I'll get is a photo?" He'd been imagining a big golden statue that resembled an Oscar, and now he felt somehow deflated.

Greer just shook her head. "All right, people. Time to get cracking. Daniel, let's go."

She grabbed her jacket and stepped out of the RV.

At 2:00 a.m., the morning air was cold and crisp. Overhead, stars twinkled, reminding her of the night she and Daniel had viewed the cosmos through his telescope. Greer's breath billowed out in a cloud of steam. Though the air was cold, the morning was expected to be clear and sunny, unlike the year she'd been Rose Queen and temperature were in the forties.

"What happens if it starts to rain?" Daniel asked.

"You get wet." Greer skirted a drill team of high school girls in yellow-and-green uniforms. "Stop worrying. There is no rain in the forecast. My dad once told me that we have a deal with God. If January first falls on Sunday, the parade is moved to Monday, and for that God promised not to rain on the parade."

"Are you kidding me?" Daniel said.

"Considering the parade has been rain-free except just a couple times, I think we should take it on faith."

The Rose Bowl parking lot was pandemonium.

Yellow school buses opened up to drop off high school bands from all over the country. Trailers let out high-stepping purebred horses decked out in luxurious silver saddles and riders just as ornately decorated. A line of antique cars heading the parade contained the grand marshal and various dignitaries. When they were given the signal, the first of the bands would fall into formation, and one by one the floats, the other bands and various horse teams would join in, slowly moving out of the lot to the staging area at San Gabriel Boulevard and Huntington Drive.

Daniel looked stunned. "How does anyone make sense of all this?"

"Stop worrying. That's my job." She hurried him into the float tent. The huge entry flaps were thrown back and floats were pulling out, ready to get into position. "Rod Ortega knows his job, so stop thinking about it. Just stand on the float and look pretty."

Every year brought a thrill of excitement for Greer. The parade never grew old.

She walked a few steps, suddenly aware that Daniel wasn't with her. She turned back to find him standing still, just staring at the bedlam. She went back and grabbed his hand. "Come on. You don't have time for this." She dragged him toward the float.

Rod was already there. Nick and Michelle stood on their dance floor, waiting. Cecile Holloway stood at her station, looking fabulous in a dark green pantsuit and seeming happy. The parade wouldn't start for six hours, yet excitement rippled through the waiting floats.

"My first Rose Parade," Cecile gushed when Daniel took his spot next to her.

Knowing it was time to start moving, Greer wished everyone luck and jumped down from the float. She found Chelsea and Rachel waiting for her.

"Come on," Rachel said. "Mom and Dad are saving our seats."

They had seats in the grandstand just beneath the TV booth where the parade commentators were housed. At times like this, Greer wished she had roller skates to get her to the grandstand.

Slowly the parade reached its starting point. In a couple of hours, another Tournament of Roses parade would be underway.

Greer and her sisters half trotted down the dark side streets until they reached Colorado Boulevard and then eventually the grandstands with the commentators' booth at the very top.

Greer's parents waved, and slowly she and her sisters made their way up the side steps and eased over to sit with their parents. Greer leaned against her father and closed her eyes. She still had two more hours to wait, but in the meantime, she could take a quick nap. Her dad folded an arm around her and pulled a blanket over her shoulders.

The beginning of the parade was still a few blocks away, and people stirred restlessly. Chelsea had volunteered to sneak into the area where the banners were held so she could see which floats won the trophies, but Greer told her no. She wanted to be surprised.

Suddenly the crowd jumped to its feet. The sound car and the pace car turned onto Colorado Boulevard, followed by the banner with the year's theme. After the banner was the tournament president with the opening ceremonies. Music swelled with the marching band and a flyover by a B-2 Stealth Bomber. The parade had begun.

Floats, marching bands, horse clubs and antique cars moved past, followed by the grand marshal. Greer clapped hard and then tried not to cry when the float from Brocade Industries moved past with no trophy banner. She crossed her fingers. More bands, more horses, a cavalry detachment from Arizona and then Logan's float. No banner. He hadn't won the Sweepstakes Trophy. She clenched her hands.

Chelsea leaned toward her. "Brian Kellerman won't be gloating this year."

More bands, more horses and the Rose Queen and her court floated by. Daniel's float was turning the corner, and Greer squinted, trying to see. No banner.

Daniel hadn't won his trophy, either. She hoped he wasn't too disappointed.

"There's always next year," her father said, patting her knee. "But look. Your float for Trident Airlines won the President's Trophy."

Greer swallowed her disappointment. She had so wanted Daniel to win his trophy, but she understood the competition better than he did. Every float was so beautiful that the judges had a hard time choosing. She knew Logan was probably seriously disappointed, as well. Now the two of them would have to work out their wager.

As she sat down, she pulled out her notebook. An idea for a new float had been germinating in her mind since Daniel had taken her to Griffith Park to show her the night sky. She'd done a few preliminary sketches, but the last part suddenly fell into place, the idea finally emerging in its entirety. She sketched quickly, her pencil moving across the drawing pad with precision as she focused on a float made up of a constellation of stars against a blanket of deep purple. She penciled in colors as her mind revealed them. Suddenly she realized the parade had ended and the crowds were breaking up.

"Do you think they were seriously disappointed?" Greer's mother asked. Virginia sat on a cushion, her coat tight around her. Next to her, her father shaded his face with a hand as he watched the street.

"I'm sure Daniel was. I don't know about Logan... yet." She'd probably find out. Neither of them winning the bet was probably a first and a humbling experience for Logan. She felt a little sorry for him anyway.

"Daniel wants to sponsor a float next year, too," Virginia continued. "He asked me a couple of days ago. And Logan called and decided you need to design his float for next year. Apparently Brian wasn't very easy to work with."

"We'll work it out." Greer closed her notebook. The design she'd finished was for Daniel only because he was the man she'd come to love. Logan would get her best effort, but her passion would be for Daniel alone.

She smiled as she stood and worked her way toward the steps. She would meet Daniel at the float.

A few rows down, Greer saw Daniel's parents sitting with several men who looked enough like Daniel to be his brothers. His sisters, Nina and Lola, he'd told her, had decided to watch the parade on television rather than face the crowds. She waved and they all waved back. Two of the young men studied her thoroughly, their gazes so piercing she wanted to run away from them.

Daniel watched Greer as she pushed through the crowds mobbing the line of floats. The parade had been the best time he'd ever had, but seeing Greer reminded him that he'd discovered more than just the thrill of the parade. He'd found Greer, and his heart swelled with love for her. She was so beautiful, so poised, so talented. He was so deeply in love with her.

She stopped to speak to Rod Ortega. A little girl

Daniel assumed was his daughter jumped up and down.

"Daniel," Cecile Holloway said. "I want to thank you for this gift."

He turned to her. "Thank you for being my partner."

Cecile smiled, her features lighting up with pleasure and showing a hint of the young woman she'd once been. She was still beautiful, but age had added a glow to her. "My husband's here. We've been married for fifty-five years."

An elderly man approached. He bent down to kiss Cecile's cheek. "The limo is just over a block away."

"Thank you, Frank," Cecile said, stroking his cheek. She turned back to Daniel. "You need to tell her."

He glanced away from Greer to Cecile.

"Tell her you love her, young man," Cecile said gently. "I've been watching the two of you, and if you don't, you're going to let the best thing that ever happened to you get away."

"I…" He stopped, not certain what to say.

"She loves you, too." Cecile pushed him. "Now go get her. Give the tabloids something new to gossip about. They love weddings."

As he walked toward Greer, he thought about their night watching the stars, the day they'd decorated her house, their dinner with his parents. As each scene replayed itself in his mind, he knew that he'd finally found the woman he would love the rest of his life.

Greer turned to him as he approached. He grabbed

her hands and saw the look of passion deep in her eyes. Without preamble, he kissed her and said, "I love you."

Greer went still, her gaze searching his face. "Really? Even though you didn't win your trophy?"

He held her tight against him. "I love you."

She rested her head against his shoulder. "I love you, too."

After the parade, the floats were lined up along Sierra Madre Avenue, where they'd be for the next week for people to view. Greer stood to one side while Daniel's cameraman shouldered the camera for a panoramic view of the line of floats. Crowds drifted down the street and sidewalk. Many of the people took photos. So few knew what really went into the procedure of creating a float, and Greer would never say anything. Let them all believe in the magic.

Her gaze slid back to Daniel. He made her feel safe and warm within the cocoon of his love. She felt like the butterflies on his float, stretching and changing from the lowly caterpillar to the majestic monarch butterfly.

"That was an experience," Daniel said. He kissed her, and she grinned at him. He'd just finished a segment for his next show detailing his parade experience, his disappointment over the lack of a trophy and his hopes and dreams for next year. He and Logan had decided they would each donate the maximum amount to their favorite charities.

"What happens to the floats now?" he asked.

"At the end of the week," Greer answered, "we'll take them all back to the warehouse, break them down and throw away what can't be salvaged and recycled for next year."

"And the cycle starts again."

"Yes, isn't it exciting?" And every year she would work from concept to finished float and then watch the parade again. She could hardly wait. The difference was that now Daniel would be at her side.

"What's the theme for next year?" Daniel asked.

"The Hope of the Future." The theme had been announced just hours ago, and she already knew how the float she'd designed for him for next year would be reworked. She needed to make a few adjustments, but she saw the future in the stars. The meaning would be personal for both of them.

"How do you feel about getting married on next year's float?" she asked.

"Are you proposing to me?"

"Yes. Yes, I am." She felt a silly grin spread across her face. More adjustments to the float would be needed, but she do could them in her sleep.

Joy lit his face. "Then I accept. Yes. Yes, let's get married on next year's float."

"I can't promise a trophy, but I can promise a moment that will stay with us for a lifetime."

"Logan and I amended our contest. Next year it will just be any trophy."

Greer simply laughed, ideas spinning through her as she mentally calculated distribution and weight. "Are you sorry about not winning?"

Daniel slid his arm around her and pulled her to him. "Winning a trophy wasn't as important as winning you."

She leaned against him with a sigh as he kissed her.

* * * * *

Lavish destination weddings set the stage for romance and desire…

KIMANI™ ROMANCE

USA TODAY Bestselling Author
**NANA MALONE
JAMIE POPE**

NANA MALONE
JAMIE POPE

A *Vow* of
SEDUCTION

This collection features two stories from fan-favorite authors. Pack your bags and get ready to board the wedding express as these couples journey from the Hamptons to Costa Rica, from forbidden pleasure to sweet bliss…

Available September 2016!

"The story flows well, without being predictable. The dialogue is strong and the characters are endearing, funny and well rounded."
—*RT Book Reviews* on *SURRENDER AT SUNSET* by Jamie Pope

HARLEQUIN®
™ www.Harlequin.com

KPNMJP465

A seduction worth waiting for...

MARTHA
KENNERSON

TEMPTING
the
HEIRESS

Felicia Blake's fantasies about Griffin Kaile didn't include discovering
that he's the biological father of the baby girl she's been asked to
raise. Felicia is reluctant to jump from passion to instant family. Can
Griffin show her that their breathtaking chemistry occurs only once
in a lifetime?

THE BLAKE SISTERS

Available September 2016!

"Kennerson uses amazing imagery, which stimulates the senses and
makes readers feel like they are in the novel."
—*RT Book Reviews* on *SEDUCING THE HEIRESS*

www.Harlequin.com

KPMK468

REQUEST YOUR FREE BOOKS!

2 FREE NOVELS
PLUS 2 FREE GIFTS!

KIMANI™
ROMANCE

Love's ultimate destination!

YES! Please send me 2 FREE Harlequin® Kimani™ Romance novels and my 2 FREE gifts (gifts are worth about $10). After receiving them, if I don't wish to receive any more books, I can return the shipping statement marked "cancel." If I don't cancel, I will receive 4 brand-new novels every month and be billed just $5.44 per book in the U.S. or $5.99 per book in Canada. That's a savings of at least 16% off the cover price. It's quite a bargain! Shipping and handling is just 50¢ per book in the U.S. and 75¢ per book in Canada.* I understand that accepting the 2 free books and gifts places me under no obligation to buy anything. I can always return a shipment and cancel at any time. Even if I never buy another book, the two free books and gifts are mine to keep forever.

168/368 XDN GH4P

Name	(PLEASE PRINT)
Address	Apt. #
City	State/Prov.	Zip/Postal Code

Signature (if under 18, a parent or guardian must sign)

Mail to the **Reader Service:**

IN U.S.A.: P.O. Box 1867, Buffalo, NY 14240-1867
IN CANADA: P.O. Box 609, Fort Erie, Ontario L2A 5X3

Want to try two free books from another line?
Call 1-800-873-8635 or visit www.ReaderService.com.

* Terms and prices subject to change without notice. Prices do not include applicable taxes. Sales tax applicable in N.Y. Canadian residents will be charged applicable taxes. Offer not valid in Quebec. This offer is limited to one order per household. Not valid for current subscribers to Harlequin® Kimani™ Romance books. All orders subject to credit approval. Credit or debit balances in a customer's account(s) may be offset by any other outstanding balance owed by or to the customer. Please allow 4 to 6 weeks for delivery. Offer available while quantities last.

Your Privacy—The Reader Service is committed to protecting your privacy. Our Privacy Policy is available online at www.ReaderService.com or upon request from the Reader Service.

We make a portion of our mailing list available to reputable third parties that offer products we believe may interest you. If you prefer that we not exchange your name with third parties, or if you wish to clarify or modify your communication preferences, please visit us at www.ReaderService.com/consumerchoice or write to us at Reader Service Preference Service, P.O. Box 9062, Buffalo, NY 14240-9062. Include your complete name and address.

KROM15

SPECIAL EXCERPT FROM

HARLEQUIN®

KIMANI
ROMANCE

*Reality show producer Amelia Marlow has a score
to settle with sexy Nate Reyes—and buying him at a
bachelor auction promises sweet satisfaction. But the
forty hours of community service Nate owes soon turns
into sensual and sizzling overtime... Through sultry
days and even hotter nights, Nate's surprised to find
Amelia is slowly turning his "no complications wanted"
attitude into intense attraction. And he soon discovers
that he'll do anything to prove that there's only one
perfect place for Amelia—in his arms!*

*Read on for a sneak peek at
HIS SOUTHERN SWEETHEART, the next exciting
installment in Carolyn Hector's
ONCE UPON A TIARA series!*

"You're all cloak and dagger." Nate nodded at the way
she held the menu in front of her face. "Unless you need
glasses.

The way she frowned was cute. The corners of her
mouth turned down and her bottom lip poked out. A
shoe made direct contact with his shin. "My eyesight is
perfect."

"Not just your eyesight." Nate cocked his head to get a
glimpse of the hourglass curve of her shape.

"Does your cheesy machismo usually work on women?"

Nate flashed a grin. "It worked on you last week." He regretted the words the second before he finished the *K* in week. Amelia's foot came into contact with his shin again. "Sorry. Chalk this up to being nervous."

Amelia settled back against the black leather booth. "You're supposed to be nervous?"

"Who wouldn't be?" Nate relaxed in his seat. "You breeze into town and drop a wad of cash on me just to make me do work for what you could have hired someone else to do, and much more cheaply, too."

The little flower in the center of her white spaghetti-strap top rose up and down. Even through the flicker of the flame bouncing off the deep maroon glass candleholder, he caught the way her cheeks turned pink.

"Let's say I don't trust anyone around town to do the work for me."

Don't miss HIS SOUTHERN SWEETHEART
by Carolyn Hector, available October 2016
wherever Harlequin® Kimani Romance™
books and ebooks are sold!

Copyright © 2016 by Carolyn Hall

KPEXP0916